WHAT
DARKNESS
REMAINS

thirteen tales of the supernatural and unknown

ANDREW M. SEDDON

To Olivia: For many reasons.

And in memory of Lady Silver (c. 2007-2017)—Buggle, we miss you and hope and pray that you are healed and restored and enjoying life in a much better and happier place.

Thanks as always to Werner Lind and Collen Drippé for unfailingly helpful critiques and comments. To Pierre Comtois for improving the three stories that appeared in "Fungi". To Grace Bridges for editing, formatting, and another awesome cover design. And to Fr. Samuel Spiering for assistance with Latin. All of you have helped to make this a better book.

Several stories have been previously published:

"What Darkness Remains," *Fungi #21*, Pierre Comtois, Ed., 2013: Fungoid Press, p. 207-121.

"Hounded By Night," *Fungi #20*, Pierre Comtois, Ed., 2011: Fungoid Press, p.83-88.

"Sonata For Piano, Four Hands," *Fungi #22*, Pierre Comtois, Ed., 2015: Virtual Bookworm, p. 65-68.

"Red Molly" in *Just Desserts*, J.A. Campbell and Rebecca McFarland Kyle, eds, WolfSinger Publications, 2016, p. 66-77.

All have been revised for this publication.

Notes: *"Dies Irae"* is a sequel to the story "Princess of Darkness" by Frederick Cowles (1900-1949) available in *The Night Wind Howls, The Complete Supernatural Stories*, Ash-Tree Press: 1999. I have been unable to locate the copyright holder for Cowles' stories despite contacting the publisher. I offer *"Dies Irae"* in homage to Frederick Cowles, a fine writer of supernatural tales, and will be happy to make any further acknowledgments as may be needed or requested.

Acknowledgements are also due to H.P. Lovecraft for creating the Plateau of Leng, and to Frank Belknap Long for creating Liao and the Hounds of Tindalos, as used in "Hounded By Night." The quotations in this story are from Long's story "The Hounds of Tindalos" (*Weird Tales*, 1929).

contents

one

CHACO

The stones of the ancient wall shone dimly in the pale, milky light of the nearly-full moon, as if lit by a gentle radiance from within. The night was still, almost preternaturally so; only the crunch of Ayska's hiking boots on the desert rubble and the panting of her German Shepherd, Shackleton, keeping pace beside her, disturbed a silence so deep that it might have always existed inviolate.

What a stark contrast to the day, when the sun blistered from a brittle-blue sky, and chattering tourists, students, and archaeologists poked through the dry brush and prowled the decaying ruins, their cameras and smartphones clicking a ceaseless, annoying toccata! But now, the long-abandoned chambers and kivas belonged only to her and Shackleton.

And yet...was she truly alone?

She could almost sense the presence of the vanished builders, the enigmatic people who had fashioned these great, scattered complexes and then disappeared some eight hundred years ago. The ancestors of the Pueblo Indians, so the experts said.

But *who* were they? What did they believe? Why did they leave their elaborately fabricated cities? And were these massive constructions really cities at all, or did they serve some other forgotten and unfathomable, purpose?

Shackleton, not perplexed by unanswerable ruminations, trotted contentedly, ears erect, yet at ease. Ayska was the only human here. Shackleton would have alerted, otherwise.

Yet she couldn't shake off a nagging sensation of…what?

Nothing she could put a name to.

She'd come to this inhospitable wasteland of canyons and mesas to escape——to seek solace from a failed marriage, the unexpected loss of her job, and the disapproval of family members who blamed her for both.

Blamed *her*! It had only been a weekend fling with an employee in her department during a company trip to Vegas. No big deal. It would have blown over—and nobody would have been the wiser—if the fathead had kept his mouth shut and not bragged to the jealous tart in accounting who brought it to the attention of Ayska's uptight boss who was probably no stranger to chance encounters himself.

It wasn't fair!

She clenched her fists.

Her husband had said it was the last straw, although he hadn't exactly been an angel himself.

And to make matters worse, friends whom she'd thought would stand by her, hadn't. They'd pretended to be horrified—in this day and age! Hypocrites, the lot of them.

All she had was Shackleton. A dog.

More than a dog—her best, and apparently only, friend.

She relaxed her hands and reached down to ruffle his ears.

"You'd never leave me, would you, boy?"

His eyes shone with the tapetal reflex that made his night vision so much better than hers.

She knew he wouldn't. To Shackleton, she could do no wrong. He would always accept her as she was; greet her with wagging tale; never act as if she was less than the greatest person in the world.

And she was strong. She'd handle her problems on her own, just as she always had.

They rounded a corner beside an open plaza bathed in moonlight. Ayska abruptly halted. Because there, in the shadow cast by the wall, was there a human figure -?

She blinked, and glanced down at Shackleton. Head cocked, the dog was staring in the opposite direction, into the desert. Probably hearing the faint movement of some night creature, or catching its scent. Perhaps one of the coyotes she'd spotted skulking around earlier in the day, scavenging for trash. No coyote in its right mind would take on Shackleton. Neither did people, typically giving the big dog a wide berth.

She peered back into the shadow, wondering if her eyes were just playing tricks.

No, there was definitely a figure. Man or woman, it was impossible to tell. Long hair. She couldn't make out clothing, but somehow knew—or sensed—that this wasn't a modern person. The form seemed insubstantial, and perhaps—she wasn't certain—she could even make out the lines of building stones through it.

She shivered.

Belatedly, she remembered the flashlight slung at her hip, reached for it, thumbed the switch, and shone the beam toward the figure.

Nothing. Only stones.

She crossed over to where it had stood. The desert sand was unmarked.

Swearing softly under her breath, she turned off the flashlight, returned it to her belt, and waited for her night vision to return.

Nerves.

Visual hallucinations.

The sign of an overstressed and overtired mind.

"Shackleton!" she called as the dog had wandered away. "Let's go, boy."

What would she do without him? He was her lifeline. She bent over to hug him as he returned.

Tonight, as they had for several nights, they'd lie side by side in the camper shell on her pick-up truck, parked inconspicuously in a gully. He snored, but not as badly as her ex had.

She spent most of the next day sitting in the shade of a cottonwood, sipping iced tea and alternately thinking and reading a cliché-riddled supernatural thriller. The type that her ex had despised; oh how she'd loathed the supercilious expression that he'd affect when he'd catch her reading such "garbage"! She smiled to herself. He hadn't been so smirky when he'd found out what she'd done to his collection of legal novels…

Shackleton didn't care about her reading habits; he gnawed his way through a stash of rawhides while keeping a wary eye open for desert wildlife and snapping at pesky flies.

When evening came, the urge to return to the ruins tantalized her until it became overwhelming, like a bad case of restless legs crescendoing until the urge to move became impossible to resist. And yet she wasn't sure why the compulsion possessed her. Was it mere curiosity? The need to reassure herself that she wasn't losing her mind? Or just the desire to walk in the coolness after having been inactive all day?

She headed out as the clouds lost the bright hues of sunset and faded to gray shreds. Shackleton didn't object; he'd always been more active late in the day. The sinking sun picked out gold and silver highlights in his fur, and she thought he seemed even more handsome than usual.

By the time she reached the ancient ruins, night had draped a black shroud over them, a darkness that the cloud-wrapped full moon could only partly offset.

The full moon. She gazed upwards at the Earth's companion, at the limit of its progression along the horizon. Now it would retrace its eight and one half year journey before traveling back again in a cycle that the

Chaco builders had known and recorded in stone, carving spirals that marked the moon's progress.

But why? Knowledge of the solar cycle was common to all ancient cultures—identifying the solstices and equinoxes helped them regulate their seasons and years. But as for the moon, what role did the more complicated lunar cycle play as its rising and setting traveled up and down the horizon in a cycle that required generations of observation to determine?

Perhaps it was only her imagination, but she thought the moon more chilly-white than usual as it peeked from between the thin, tattered clouds.

Last night, she'd been expecting nothing but a casual walk. Tonight...tonight felt different. The darkened sand dunes could have been the surface of an alien planet, the jagged walls the ruins of some gloomy mythological fortress——but everything slightly tenuous, as if veiled, or wavering on the edge of reality.

Her fingertips tingled as she walked alongside the wall, her eyes scanning every patch of shadow, occasionally darting towards Shackleton to see if the German Shepherd was alerting to anything.

Breathing.

She spun on her heel, hand reaching for the bear spray that she always carried for self-defense. It worked well on people too; while Shackleton was normally a more-than-adequate deterrent, she'd had to use the spray a time or two when she'd been out without the dog.

Nobody. She gave a nervous laugh as she realized the hoarse, rapid breathing was her own. The sound brought back a recent memory.

"Some people say there's something wrong there," a wheezing old Zuni man had told her when she'd arrived at Chaco.

"What do you mean?" she'd asked.

"They say that those people—the old ones—tried to control the forces of nature. But something went wrong. Perhaps they wanted more power than anyone should have. Perhaps they used them for dark reasons. But that is why they left, why they disappeared. So they say."

So as not to offend him, she'd waited until he was out of sight before breaking into laughter. Ancient magic, indeed!

Well, she didn't believe in any of that. Not the stuff of legend, not what her parents had believed or what they taught in church, not the supernatural, and certainly not what she read in her books, no matter how much she enjoyed them.

But the Chacoans *had* believed in something. Up on the mesa lay mounds of pottery sherds. Broken, claimed the archaeologists, so the living could no longer use the vessels. Broken to be sent into the afterlife.

And Chaco itself had been broken—the doors bricked up, the roofs of the kivas removed and burned. And the people themselves had wandered off into the rugged, unforgiving desert, leaving their magnificent creation to the mercy of vandals, weather, scavengers, and rodents.

Forgotten powers?

Forbidden knowledge?

Tales to titillate gullible tourists. She smiled to herself. She was a modern woman, a material one, and yet…yet despite herself, sometimes she wondered.

Behind her, the sandstone cliffs reared into the night sky. The moonlight picked out cracks and crevices, creating the illusion that a thousand half-hidden faces watched her, following her every movement, while the wind swishing around corners was a multitude of whispering voices…

Her fingers folded around an angle of brick and she halted at the end of the wall. Did she really want to round the corner and see what was there, in the moonlight and the shadow? She could retrace her steps, return to the camper, curl up with Shackleton and her book…

Something told her that was the prudent, sensible course of action.

Go back, whispered an inner voice. *It's not worth it. Go back.*

But another part of her answered, *If you do, you'll never know.*

Never know.

Never.

Know.

She took a deep breath, braced herself, and swung around the angle of the wall.

The figure stood in the same location. But it was clearer tonight, and definitely a man, wearing a loincloth, with a fabric band tied around his forehead. He carried a staff which glittered blue at its tip—inlaid with turquoise, she supposed.

His other hand was extended towards her.

She moved closer.

His eyes were dark, hooded, downcast. She couldn't make out the expression on his face.

Something tugged on the cuff of her jeans; Shackleton, pulling her back. She reached down to push the dog away.

The man didn't move, transfixed at the intersection of light and dark.

His extended hand was open.

What did it mean, that hand?

Did he—whatever he was—want to leave whatever place or state of being he now inhabited, and return to the real world his ancestors had once occupied? By taking his hand, could she pull him back to the tangible?

Or, more likely, was he inviting her to leave her devastated world of shattered hopes and crumbled dreams, and follow him to where—she imagined—those ancients, some of them, anyway, had gone?

She shook her head. What was she thinking? Doorways to other dimensions? The stuff of science fiction.

Shackleton whined—not the eager sound he made when he wanted to play ball, but the low, imploring whine that said, "I don't like this."

"Hush," she said, more harshly than she intended. "Be quiet."

For a moment she hesitated, aware of her sweaty palms. The whole thing was crazy. Almost, she turned away. But something inside urged her on. And what had she to lose? She wasn't afraid of the unknown, or of taking a chance—and what was life but one chance after another? Besides, if it was a hallucination, a projection of her subconscious—or even a ghost, not that she believed in *them*—her hand would pass right through it. She stepped forward, raising her arm as she did so.

Shackleton growled, his hackles standing spikily erect.

"Stay!" she commanded sharply.

A cloud slipped across the face of the moon, and the figure appeared to retreat into the fabric of the wall. She lunged ahead and clasped the offered hand, gasping at the icy cold of the fingers.

She tried to pull back, but the shadow drew her in.

It was only at the last moment that she glimpsed the eyes, as vacant and hollow as Chaco's gaping windows, set in a face that, if it had once been human, now imaged the same desolation as the interminable, featureless, barren rooms. And she understood that the old Zuni was right—and why Chaco had been sealed by the survivors fleeing the ancient evil.

She opened her mouth, but it was too late to scream.

Shackleton, alone by the wall, threw back his head and howled. But his only reply was the sighing of the wind among the tumbled stones and the whispering of the disturbed desert sand.

two

WHAT DARKNESS REMAINS

The pope handled the age-darkened parchment gingerly, as if afraid that the slightest touch would cause it to crumble into dust. His gaze passed from the lines of ancient Latin script to the cracked wooden chest that sat next to it on his desk, and then to the two men standing across from him.

One wore a suit and tie; the other, the ordinary dress of a cardinal—a black cassock with scarlet piping, a scarlet sash, and zucchetto.

"Where did this come from?" he asked.

The Vatican Secretary of State cleared his throat. "It was discovered by a building contractor working in the catacombs beneath St. Peter's, Your Holiness."

"His company was hired to help with renovations and stabilization," added the other man, an archaeologist. "The chest was concealed in a hollow behind a number of loose stones. We immediately brought it to the attention of St. Peter's Administrator, and he notified the cardinal."

"I was told only that a significant discovery had been made," the pope said. He regarded the two men for a moment, then, indicating the document, asked, "Did either of you read it?"

"Only the first few lines," the archaeologist admitted. "Enough to see that it was important…and unusual."

"With respect, Your Holiness," the cardinal said, "I don't think this is something that you need to spend your valuable time on…"

"Let me be the judge of that," the pope said, firmly but without rancor. He motioned toward a pair of chairs.

"Please be seated, both of you." He adjusted his glasses and began reading.

To His Holiness, Pope Clement V, from Etienne Gerrard de Charny, Knight of the Temple and captive of Philip, King of France, greetings.

I have done what I thought necessary. Let Your Holiness judge whether or not it was done aright. I send you, by the hand of a trusted friend, this chest and what it contains as proof that what I write is true.

Unless Your Holiness intervenes, my captivity shall be ended only by my death—thus is decreed by King Philip to be the fate of loyal Knights of the Temple.

Death holds no terrors for me. Yet still I fear. I fear great darkness in the courts of the king. I fear that the evil that I fight is not truly gone…that it may yet again rear its loathsome head. And I fear that the summons to serve will come to me again, and I not be able to answer it. And if not I, and if my brother knights all be dead or imprisoned—since even our Grand Master has now been made captive by the king's order—who will?

"Interesting," concluded the pope non-commitally. "Do we know anything of this Gerrard de Charny?"

The archaeologist shook his head. "Not to my knowledge. There was, however, a Geoffrey de Charny who was Preceptor of Normandy and who was burned alongside Grand Master Jacques de Molay in 1314. This Gerrard may have been a relative. That's only a guess, mind you."

"Well, let's see what Gerrard has to say, shall we?"

It happened just over a twelve-month ago. Finding myself unable to sleep, I had gone for a walk. Reciting the Psalms as I went, I was paying but little attention to my surroundings, conscious only that I had taken the road that ran near the sea-cliffs.

And so I was startled by a noise as of a mighty, roaring wind, and looking up beheld a disc of flame, burning with many colors, descend from the night sky. The sea erupted as it swallowed it, boiling and churning and hurling great gouts of water toward the stars which faded behind a veil of billowing steam. The hot wave of its passing bade fair to tear the mantle from my shoulders.

I stood on the cliffs, watching as the mist dissipated and the roaring and hissing quietened. Deep below the surface of the waters a dull red glow lingered, gradually fading like dying embers. Finally the sea calmed, until once more there was nothing but inky black waves lapping on the shore.

And in the moonlight—for the moon was full and the night bright—I saw diminutive figures on the narrow strip of beach where there had been none before.

I sensed, I know not how, that evil had come to the land, and my right hand traced where once a red cross had emblazoned my mantle; the cross that had marked me as a Knight of the Temple, one whose life was not his own.

The Order had been dissolved, brought low by the lies and machinations of sinful men, but I intended to keep the vows that I had taken.

"Quite descriptive, don't you think?" the pope said.

"Evocative," the archaeologist concurred.

The cardinal wiped his palms on his cassock. "Disturbing, I'd say."

When next I saw them some days later, it was in the castle, as they presented themselves to the count, although at first, I realized not who they were.

I arrived to find the count in audience with a group of strangers—tall, well-built men, handsomely dressed, honorable to all appearance, and yet something about them jarred my spirit, as if somehow the appearance did not match the reality.

I positioned myself to watch and listen.

The count, a man somewhat younger than myself, whose body was strong and hair untouched by gray, regarded them with curiosity. "Where are you from, and why are you here?"

The tallest man replied, "From far away. We seek sanctuary."

It was vague. Far too vague. The count must have thought the same, for he motioned the stranger to continue.

"Our vessel sank," the same individual—their spokesman—answered. "We need somewhere to live."

His lips…did his lips move?

The count's expression radiated suspicion; he tugged on his beard, as he always did when deep in thought.

"We can pay," the stranger said, extending an arm. Jewels glittered in his palm. The count extended his own hand, palm up, and the stranger let the jewels fall onto it.

The count held them to his eyes. "A king's ransom!" he exclaimed.

"There are more," the stranger said. "As many as you desire."

It was then, as the count's expression mutated from suspicion to covetousness and while the stranger emanated satisfaction, that a wave of unease swept over me—nausea, weakness, and a sudden dimming of vision. For a moment I felt like a man in the desert, bereft of water, the burning sun about to cast him senseless to the equally burning sand.

The sensation passed, yet I shivered, feeling that the evil in the room was almost palpable. Was I the only one who sensed it?

"We are glad to welcome you among us," the count said.

I shouldered my way through a knot of onlookers.

"My lord," I called. "I would speak with you."

The count scowled at the interruption, then his eyes lit upon me. "Gerrard de

Charny! I heard you were dead!"

"I very nearly was."

"Come closer." The count rose and studied me as I approached. "You still look like death."

"Not that bad, surely," I replied, my hand rising instinctively to the scar that ran across my forehead and down my cheek, placed there by a Saracen sword.

"Near enough," he replied. "Now, what brings you here?"

I shrugged. "Where else is there for me to go?"

He nodded understanding. "A man without an order...why didn't you join the Hospitallers?"

"Who would take a man that looks like death?" I replied, shaking my head. "My fighting days are over. My brothers may spare me a small piece of land..."

"It is well." The count motioned. "Did you have else to say?"

I cast a sideways glance at the strangers, and paused, suddenly unsure of my words. What was I to say? That I had seen unusual figures on a beach at night? A momentary glimpse of something that might—or might not—be real?

I lowered my voice. "The strangers..."

"What about them?" snapped the count, never a man to appreciate unsolicited advice.

"I don't think...they're not what they appear."

The count's brows furrowed. "Speak plainly, man!"

"There's something evil about them," I said.

He glowered. "Nonsense! They are perfectly normal men with good intentions. Why would they offer me these..." and he held out his handful of glittering jewels, "if they meant harm?"

Why indeed?

The count turned to the bishop, who was standing nearby, examining a large gem of his own.

"Do you sense anything amiss?"

"Nothing," the bishop replied, not taking his eyes off the jewel.

"What do you say to that?" the count demanded. "Would you argue with a prince of the church?"

I had no answer; the count dismissed me with a curt motion, and I could read in his expression what he thought of me. We were distant kin, yet I had been a member of an

13

order that had been discredited, accused—though falsely—of the rankest heresies and blasphemies. Because of our blood ties, the count would tolerate my presence in his territories if I remained quiet and inconspicuous. But if I crossed him...

I slunk out, leaving him to discourse with the seven strangers.

Seven.

The same number of figures that I had seen on the beach.

It could not, surely, be a coincidence.

But what was I to do?

Never before had I doubted the evidence of my own senses, yet what if my injuries had left me with wounds deeper than mere scars? I suffered from headaches, and the occasional fit. Could I rely on what my eyes told me? What if the problem lay with me and not with the strangers?

There was nothing I could do.

I decided to wait and watch.

The pope paused, laid the parchment down, reached for a glass of water, and sipped.

"Gerrard sounds as if he was not quite in his right mind," the cardinal commented. "Assuming, of course that this missive is meant to be taken seriously, and not as a work of fiction."

"The Latin is quite fluent," the pope said. "He must have been an educated man."

"Which does not preclude mental illness," the cardinal countered.

"Admittedly. But let's not be hasty." The pope set the glass aside and retrieved the parchment.

I returned to my family's property. My eldest brother was none too glad to see me, but grudgingly allowed me a hut on the edge of his lands, and bread enough to sustain me.

A place to sleep, and a place to pray; that was all I needed.

And when I wasn't doing either, I kept myself apprised of events at the count's court.

It wasn't long before I sensed a change.

Even though I had been overseas for years and heard little news in that time, I was sure the changes were due to the arrival of the strangers.

The count had always been a man of moderation and temperance…at least, to the extent that any nobleman could approach those virtues. His wife showed charity for the poor, his children were well-mannered. But now his dress became more extravagant, his table richer, his armour fine enough to rival a king's, his horses the best that money could buy. His eyes wandered, and comely young women were seen entering and leaving his chambers.

His wife positively gleamed with rings and necklaces of precious stones. Each handmaiden seemed to have been replaced by a dozen, and rarely did silence break the sounds of revelry in the court.

Yet for all this, the count did not appear to grow in happiness…rather, his temper worsened until displays of anger dominated his audiences. The casks of wine and barrels of ale served only to inflame his passions and increase the slothfulness that turned him from a vigorous man into a soft parody of himself. No matter what he had, he wanted more.

When he deigned to tour his territories or welcome a visiting nobleman, he comported himself like a peacock, strutting as if he were a king, and not the ruler of a minor fiefdom.

And always, one of the strangers was near at hand.

All this I saw.

But it was not until I encountered one of the count's bakers that I had my first inkling that there was more than moral evil abroad in the land.

Restless, I had been walking the fields and lanes at night, not caring where my feet took me, my gaze fixed on the stars festooning the night sky. I paid little heed to the footsteps I heard approaching, until I rounded a corner on the outskirts of the town, and saw a man slumped against the wall of a building. Perhaps a nearby shadow disappeared into the darkness, but of this I wasn't sure.

I crossed over to the man.

"Fellow, are you all right?" I shook his shoulder. "Fellow!"

15

His eyes raised, and in their unfocused depths I saw...nothing. A blankness that compelled me to take a step backwards.

Then the haunted eyes focused, and fear replaced the emptiness. But not the sharp-edged fear of acute peril. No. This was something deeper, inchoate, a fear robbed of the will to respond, lacking the energy to take action.

The baker took a gasping breath, then pushed off the wall and lurched down the street like a man half-drunk whose wits had deserted him.

And as he shambled past me, my gaze was drawn to a faint line on his temple...a thread no more than an inch long that shone harshly in the light of a nearby torch. It reminded me of nothing so much as a fresh scar. But there was no blood, no suture.

Then he was gone, and I betook myself home, perplexed.

It was perhaps two weeks later that I encountered the count, riding his stallion through the town, as I left the church where I had been praying.

"Gerrard!" he called, for once in an affable mood.

"My lord," I replied.

He leaned over, and lowered his voice. "Tell me, Gerrard, have you noticed anything amiss?"

I pondered the question. Certainly he wouldn't be asking about his own behavior.

"Amiss?" I queried. "In what way?"

"I begin to feel that I am surrounded by idiots and imbeciles!" he exclaimed. "My baker...the countess' seamstress...three of my men at arms...all of them have become useless!"

Behind him, some feet away, I caught sight of one of the strangers.

"Curious," I mused.

"It's more than curious! It's infuriating!" The affability vanished. The count waved his hand. "There's one of the cretins now! I'm tempted to ride him down with my horse!"

"Let me talk to the man." Despite the people milling about in the square it wasn't hard to see whom the count indicated. A well-built soldier was making his way through the throng, slowly, yet heedless of where he was going, like a ship plowing through the waves, making them part before it.

"If you wish."

"If I may be so bold," I said, "I still think that the strangers..."

"Say no more!" he shouted. "I will not listen to talk about my guests!" He straightened, kicked his horse's flanks, and rode off.

I hurried to catch up to the soldier. I planted myself in front of him, forcing him to stop.

"Good fellow," I began, "do you know where…"

I broke off. His face was expressionless, and his eyes held the same emptiness as had the baker's. They looked past me into a vague distance, as if I was not there. Yet surely he could see me…

He put a hand on my shoulder, pushed me aside, and continued walking. It was uncanny.

Had he screamed, cursed, begun raving, I should have thought him mad…or possessed—and that I could have understood. But the chilling silence and the lack of emotion nearly made the spirit quail within me.

I sought out the bishop. Surely he would be able to offer advice.

His servant denied me admission.

"My lord bishop isn't well," he said.

My foot in the door prevented him from closing it.

"What's the matter with him?" I asked.

The servant shook his head and glanced nervously over his shoulder. "I don't know," he whispered. "He sits and stares into the fireplace for hours on end. When he speaks—which isn't often—he repeats the same words over and over. It's as if he isn't there."

I withdrew my foot.

The bishop, the baker, the seamstress, three men at arms.

Six.

Would there be seven?

The count would not listen to me, but I could not allow myself to do nothing.

The visitors had taken up residence in the count's palace. I knew I had to begin there.

"This is nonsense, Holiness," the cardinal said. "Utter nonsense."

"I find it fascinating," the archaeologist remarked.

The cardinal gestured towards the other man. "I wager that once the professor has been able to perform a more detailed examination—perhaps with a scientific team—and radiocarbon date it, the document will be exposed as a sham." He made to rise. "Your Holiness, if I may be excused..."

"Not just yet," the pope replied, motioning for the Secretary of State to resume his seat. "Let's hear the end of the story before making a judgment."

Night had long since fallen, when, wearing a dark cloak, I concealed myself in a doorway from which I could observe the entrance.

The hours passed, and no one emerged.

I waited until dawn pinked the sky, then I returned home.

I did the same for the next five nights. Each vigil felt longer than the one before. Yet nothing happened.

It was on the sixth night that my persistence was rewarded.

The door creaked open, candlelight was quickly extinguished, and a figure emerged, followed by several others. I counted them...there were eight.

The moon was lacking only a night or two of fullness, and by its light I could tell that one of the figures was a woman...the countess. One of the strangers held her by the arm. Silently, they filed down the street. Keeping to the shadows, I followed, making sure my feet made no sound.

Soon the confines of the town were left behind, and the procession wended its way through the fields and copses of trees.

Where were they heading? I began to have a notion, and soon my suspicions were confirmed when the leading stranger turned onto the pathway toward the cliffs. It wasn't long before the murmuring surf obliterated the cries of night birds and the rustling of leaves.

By day, the beach was a cheerful oasis of sand and sea; but tonight it struck me as a place of shades and spirits. I remained on the top of the cliffs, watching and waiting and praying.

Once again, hours passed, the constellations moving slowly in their courses overhead, until finally I heard the crunch of footsteps on the path.

I flattened myself on the ground, watching from between a pair of boulders.

Two of the strangers passed by, then the countess. Her head was bare, the cowl of her cloak thrown back. She walked slowly, stiffly, her gaze fixed straight ahead. And, unless my eyes deceived me once again, a thin pink line marked her temple. Four more of the strangers passed.

As I watched them disappear into the darkness, anger welled up within me. Whether it was a righteous anger or not, I do not know. All I knew at the time was that these unholy strangers—be they men or devils—were doing something to the people of the town. My town. My people. Christian people I had vowed to protect whether in the land of Jerusalem or the provinces of France.

In my heart, I was still a knight of the Templars.

Some distance behind the others, the last stranger passed my place of concealment.

It would not be the killing of a man, I reasoned, but the killing of evil. Malicide.

If only I had girded myself with my sword before setting off for my nightly vigil!

Dismissing my regrets, I leaped to my feet, and sprang for his neck.

My hands passed right through him, and I staggered to remain upright. The words do not exist to describe the surprise—and fear—that immediately claimed me.

Yet I was a man accustomed to fear.

The stranger spun around, and this time, I lunged lower. My hands clamped around a neck. The thing squirmed, and made a mewling noise like a cat. I squeezed tighter, and felt the crunch and crackle of cartilage and bone. The figure convulsed, gave a single, faint gurgle, and went limp.

The moon, which had slid behind a cloud, reemerged, and I saw what it was I held in my grasp.

It was shorter than a man but not a dwarf. Neither was it human. Its hairless skin had the pallor of death. Lidless, oblong eyes dominated its misshapen head. Twin slits gaped where a nose should have been, and its jaws narrowed to a pointed chin. Its animal-like mouth hung open to reveal rows of small pointed teeth and a short, purple tongue.

Repulsed, I looked down and noticed that the hands lacked little fingers. A tunic that gleamed like metal in the moonlight covered its scrawny form. Its thin bones explained how easily I was able to kill it with my bare hands.

As I looked, one of its claw-like hands unclenched and a cluster of what I at first took to be gems but that turned out to be mere pebbles, streamed to the ground.

The thing was a demon, surely, and yet it was made of flesh…

With a disgusted cry, I slung the unclean monster away from me, over the cliff. Then I fell to my knees, retching like a sick child.

"Totally preposterous!" exclaimed the cardinal. "Surely you can't believe it."

"I agree that it sounds bizarre," the pope admitted. "But since we've come this far, let's continue." He shuffled the parchments. "We're near the end."

The cardinal sighed.

It took me a month to kill them all…for they were very cautious…to make them as dead as it was possible for human hands to make them.

I discovered that since I had discovered how they truly appeared, I no longer saw them as men, but as the hideous creatures they really were.

Why I was so favored to see through their false appearance, when others were not, I do not know. Not because I was holier than other men, surely. Deciding to think no more on the matter, I chose to leave the mystery to God and accept the fact that He had apparently chosen me to deal with the demonic strangers.

And so, strengthened by my faith, I slew them one by one.

Stealthily, biding my time, waiting until I could catch each one unawares.

Four I killed with the sword, another with my bare hands, and the last by poison…not a knight's manner, but the only way I could reach the thing, cowering as it was in the count's palace guarded by his men; the count to the last believing the strangers were benevolent visitors from a far country.

"I know you did it!" the count said to me, appearing at the door of my hut the day after the last of the demons perished. His sword was in his hand. "I should gut you where you stand."

"Do so, if you wish," I replied. "Kill me, and answer to God for slaying the man who delivered you from evil."

"You have robbed me of my wealth!"

"Look into the dead eyes of your wife," I countered, "and tell me who robbed you."

He snarled, but the last shreds of his faith prevented him from carrying out his threat.

"Here's your reward," he grated, throwing a handful of pebbles at my feet. "That, and the knowledge that the king will learn of this. Leave my lands, and never return."

It was the last order I obeyed from him.

"It is dated," the pope concluded, "the second of February in the year of Our Lord 1313."

"It's all too fantastic!" protested the cardinal. "Telepathic aliens posing as human beings? As I said, it *has* to be a forgery. A trick to embarrass the Church."

"If it's a forgery, it's an excellent one," the archaeologist countered. "The parchment, the ink used, the style of the writing, the seal on the chest…all appear to be authentic. Mind you, I've only had chance for a cursory examination."

"Appearances can be deceptive," the cardinal said. "And besides, aliens and UFOs are twentieth century phenomena."

The pope reached for the chest, and paused, studying a line of faded ink beneath the broken seal. Looking closer, he struggled to read the words.

"It says that the chest is not to be opened."

"Then perhaps it should remain that way," the cardinal offered.

The pope arched an eyebrow, then proceeded to raise the lid. Reaching inside, he extracted a dusty, bone-white object. Carefully, he turned the skull over in his hands, noticing the abnormally large eye sockets and the small, pointed chin with its rows of sharp teeth.

"That's not a human skull," breathed the archaeologist.

"Possibly it's an unknown hominid species," suggested the cardinal.

Reaching into the chest again, the pope extracted a second skull, a third, until six of the malformed objects sat in a row across his desk.

"Only six, not seven," the pope observed.

"Gerrard threw one off a cliff," the archaeologist reminded.

"Of course. There's another message here," said the pope, taking out a fragment of parchment from the chest. "It appears to be written in a different hand. Scribbled. Difficult to read. 'I find no guilt in him. What does it mean? I have no answer. I can do nothing. It were best that no-one else know.'"

The pope hesitated. "If I remember correctly, Clement was terminally ill at the time. The Grand Master accused him of abandoning the Templars, leaving them to their fate at Philip of France's hands. It's no wonder he couldn't face dealing with…" he motioned towards the skulls, "those."

"If Gerrard was right, King Philip may have inadvertently destroyed more than he knew," the archaeologist mused. "Not only a knightly order but Gerrard himself; the only man who knew about the threat to Earth."

"Or did Philip…or someone…or some*thing*…close to him know exactly what was being done?" the pope mused.

"You mean—" the archaeologist began.

The pope's expression was somber. "Suppose there were more of them." He picked up the parchment. "Gerrard wrote, 'I fear great darkness in the courts of the king.' They've had seven hundred years to infiltrate our society, our institutions, our governments. What if they're still here? What darkness remains?"

"Pure speculation, your Holiness!" exclaimed the cardinal. "I can't believe you're taking this seriously!"

The pope glanced at his advisor and just for a moment…for the briefest of instants…he thought he saw…

But no. It was only his imagination.

He removed his glasses and rubbed his eyes.

His Secretary of State could not be…

three

MOONSHINE CREEK

"Yes, it's a very pretty trail," said the state park ranger in answer to my question. "But I wouldn't advise starting it this late in the day."

The expression on his round face struck me as odd—a combination of warning and something else which eluded identification. Perhaps it was only my imagination—or because it was near quitting time and he wanted to go home. Whatever it was, I couldn't quite put my finger on it.

He was short and pudgy with pale, watery eyes, and gave the impression of being the type who'd prefer sitting behind a desk to venturing out into wilderness areas. He'd been collecting the money from the self-pay station—the "iron ranger"—when I drove into the parking lot and stopped beside his truck, the only other vehicle there.

"Why is that?" I asked. "The trail's not very long, is it?"

I pulled a handkerchief from my pocket and wiped off the sweat dripping down my forehead—the Florida heat and humidity was getting to me. The truth was, I was feeling somewhat drained and not up to a long hike.

"No, it's not," he replied, "but it's very easy to lose your way, especially in the dark. And frankly, I don't want to get called out in the middle of the night to come looking for you."

I studied the start of the trail. It appeared broad and well-marked.

"Is it true that it was used by moonshiners?" I wondered.

"That's why it's called Moonshine Creek," the ranger said, not bothering to hide an "isn't it obvious?" tone. He made a sweeping movement with his arm. "This was a dry county as late as the 1960s. Moonshiners operated in many secret locations. Sometimes they got caught."

His smile was curious. I didn't know what to make of it.

He made a shooting motion with his right hand.

"Thank you," I said.

"Suit yourself," he replied, obviously sensing my determination to walk the trail despite the fact that dusk wasn't far off. "Just be sure to make it out before nightfall."

"I'll be quick," I said, as he headed back to his truck, climbed in, and drove away. I was glad that he'd gone; I wasn't going to let him put me off seeing a location of historical interest.

The trail beckoned me, and I set off.

Almost immediately the woods enclosed me. The softness of fallen leaves cushioned my steps. A canopy of oaks and pines filtered the sunlight through the bright green foliage of spring, while sweet gums, wild azaleas, and magnolias vied for space in the middle height. Lower down, ferns, saw palmettos and invasive ardisia pushed through a tangle of vines and creepers. A squirrel chattered nearby, and a bluejay farther off. The air was redolent of humidity, the decay of old matter, and the fresh scent of new. A breeze fluttered down a sprinkling of last year's leaves.

The trail wound through the forest, then turned sharply downhill. I had to watch my footing so as not to trip over the numerous roots that snaked across the path. Civilization was abandoned far behind me. The sound of distant traffic faded and vanished.

The woods appeared, I supposed, much as they had when the moonshiners had been making illegal liquor seventy or so years ago during the heyday of Prohibition. I don't know why the era fascinated me so—perhaps it was because my grandfather had been a moonshiner himself, and told me tales of the secret stills, the speakeasies, and the Revenue men and Bureau of Prohibition agents—"revenoors" and "prohis" he called them—engaged in a futile war against the moonshiners, rumrunners, and bootleggers.

Grandfather had never been caught—either by good luck or—as he claimed—by virtue of his own craftiness. He had died when I was young, but the memory of his stories had never left me. Prohibition was part of my family history.

Not that there was necessarily anything romantic about the era—people died or suffered blindness or neurological problems from moonshine contaminated by lead or methanol. But perhaps there was romance in the slang of the day—of broads, dames, lookers, and canaries; dog soup and city juice; coppers and flatfeet; tin cans and flivvers; five-spots and sawbucks; dead hoofers and dollfaces.

A whitetail deer darted between the trees and vanished—and as it did so, I realized that night was falling much faster than I had anticipated. Still, the creek couldn't be much farther...

And it wasn't. I rounded another bend, and there it was, a shallow stream of crystal clear water, shining golden yellow in the fading light, trickling over a bed of sand. It wasn't wide—I could step across it easily.

I paused, wondering where along the course of the creek the moonshiners had set up their operation, as I couldn't see any remnants of their activity. Perhaps it had all rusted away, or been buried under vegetation, or been carted off. I should have thought to have asked the ranger.

Well. It was getting dark and I shouldn't linger. But even as I turned to head back, the last flicker of sunlight vanished and the woods plunged into darkness. The ranger's words echoed in my mind...but it couldn't be more than half a mile back to the parking lot. Surely I could follow the trail that far.

I hadn't taken more than a couple of steps when I heard voices from farther down the trail. I paused, then turned around again. Perhaps it was a group of hikers, and maybe one had a flashlight. Even though I was sure I'd be able to make it back without difficulty, it might be prudent to be with a group.

I stumbled ahead for a few yards, and then the amber glimmer of a light winking through the leaves arrested my attention.

The voices were louder…but they didn't sound like hikers or dog walkers—more like a group of men who'd had too much to drink. I couldn't make out the words.

I paused, wondering if I should just forget it and go back on my own. But curiosity got the better of me and I edged forward through the dark forest.

It was then that the odor reached me—a smell that reminded me of sourdough bread mixed with vomit. I had friends who made their own moonshine—legally, of course, as it was easy enough to find recipes for moonshine on the internet, as well as the equipment to set up your own home still—no need to hide in woods or caves now!—and so I recognized the pungent odor.

But why would anyone choose to make it here, in the woods, at night?

And then, as I crept forward a few more feet, I saw them—four shadowy figures partially illuminated by the light of a fire underneath what was surely a boiler. From the top protruded coils of copper pipe—condensers. Several kegs and a collection of glass jars completed the ensemble. I was sure I heard the bubbling of boiling mash and the hissing of steam.

I rubbed my eyes. I couldn't be seeing what I thought I saw, and hearing what I thought I heard, and smelling what-

Then it dawned on me. Reenactors. That had to be it!

Local folks signed on to dress up and play the part of moonshiners for the benefit of tourists like me. But why hadn't the ranger told me about them? Why had he implied that I should stay away?

A shadow of doubt crept into my supposition.

I was debating whether or not to make my presence known when an authoritative voice shouted from behind me.

"Put your hands up and stay where you are!"

My arms whipped skyward and I half-turned—

"Coppers!" exclaimed one of the shadowy figures, cursing and bolting for the woods. "Let's blouse!"

But another reached for his waistband, raised his arm, and a gunshot shattered the night.

Was it not a reenactment after all but a real raid? What had I stumbled into?

I should have dropped to the ground, but I was too paralyzed to move as gunfire erupted all around me. Shots snickered through the trees, ripping through leaves and branches.

One of the shadowy figures clutched its chest and toppled, and bullets clanked off the still and whined into the night.

With danger both in front of and behind me, my mind told me to do *something*, but my body refused to obey.

And yet I must have moved, or cried out, because one of the shadowy figures turned towards me.

The flames leaped higher, and in their light I saw, beneath a shabby fedora, something I would give anything to forget, but that I can never erase from my memory.

A cadaverous face that looked as if it had been dead for decades turned white, sightless eyes towards me. A few strands of lank hair adhered to a moldy skull, while crooked teeth hung from a maw of a mouth. Where the nose had been was only a hole set between sunken cheeks—

With a skeletal hand it raised its gun to point at my heart. I stood transfixed in horror in a moment of time that seemed endless.

And then it fired.

A couple walking their dog found me in the morning, huddled on the ground, moaning and whimpering.

My wife tells me it was three weeks before I regained lucidity.

The doctors informed me I'd suffered a bout of encephalopathy from West Nile Virus contracted from a mosquito bite.

Maybe they were right.

And the hole in my shirt, right over my heart?

Torn on a branch, concluded my wife, who sewed it.

And maybe she was right, too.

But while I have since walked many trails, all over the South, I have never gone back to Moonshine Creek.

Because still I wonder.

four

SONATA FOR PIANO, FOUR HANDS

Never in my wildest dreams could I have imagined a more unlikely setting for the awful event which I am about to relate. Quail Hollow Grange nestled in a fold between two of the gently rolling hills that shepherded the River Wye on its meandering course past the market town of Ross in Herefordshire, and could have lain there unnoticed and untouched for centuries, sheltered from the tribulations of life that swirled and eddied around it.

As my cousin Darren and I pulled into the long, curving drive shaded by weeping willows that led up to the house, I envied the good fortune that had allowed my old school friend Colinn Barnes-Roberts to acquire such an estate. It wasn't from his compositional ability, adroit as that was—nobody made a fortune from writing orchestral music—but thanks to the untimely departing to the afterlife of an uncle who had never bothered to generate his own offspring.

I sighed as we alighted and strode towards the ancient stone farmhouse, its walls festooned with ivy and wisteria, its mullioned windows glinting in the afternoon sunshine. A small brook wound its way through the grounds, fringed by rushes and moss-covered rocks, and from somewhere a wood pigeon cooed deeply.

"Some folks have all the luck," Darren commented, echoing my own sentiments.

Truth to tell, it was with some reluctance that I had accepted the invitation to visit; issued following a chance encounter in Hereford where I had played a concert. I found Colinn's scarcely concealed reputation as an amateur occultist to be somewhat off-putting. But memories of past friendship and his cordiality had carried the day.

An aged Alsatian raised his head from where he lay snoozing on the timbered porch, studied us for a moment, then gave a perfunctory *woof* and lay back down again.

"Hello, Baron," I said, giving the old guardian a pat on the head. "Good to see you again."

His tail rose once and fell with a thud.

"Darren! Roger! Welcome to my humble abode!" came a cheerful voice from an upstairs window. "Be right down."

Moments later, the front door opened, and Colinn was greeting us in his usual flamboyant manner.

"Come in, come in! It's so good to see you both. I should have had you visit sooner. Let me take your bags…"

"Good to see you too, Colinn," I replied, adding "You haven't changed a bit," before realizing that wasn't completely true.

The wide grin revealing the uneven teeth was unchanged, as was the unruly curly blond hair straying over the collar of his rumpled cardigan. His manner was pure Colinn. Yet there was something indefinably amiss. Darren must have sensed it as well, since I saw him frowning as Colinn led us upstairs to our rooms, chattering all the way.

"Must forgive the state of affairs. Housekeeper came down with a ruddy cough…been out of work all week…couldn't find anyone on short notice to replace her…"

"Don't worry, Colinn," I said as he set my overnight bag in a cheerfully appointed room. "It's delightful."

"I'll give you an hour. See you at dinner," he said, departing.

The floorboards squeaked pleasantly as I crossed to the window, parted curtains embroidered with roses and daisies, and raised the sash. A breeze laden with the scent of the countryside flowed in, something I missed, compelled as I was to spend most of my life in the noxious environs of cities. The window overlooked a wildflower garden, ablaze with a riot of hues, and beyond that a patchwork of green fields covering the hillside.

I unpacked my case, hung up my clothes, then stretched out on the bed and closed my eyes.

It hardly felt like an hour later when Darren was knocking on my door, informing me that dinner was ready. I hurried downstairs to find Colinn loading plates with lamb chops, boiled potatoes, and carrots. He motioned me to a seat at the oak table in the stone-floored dining room.

"I have a nice Welsh red wine to go with it," he said.

"Fine," I assented. He poured three glasses, and soon we were engrossed in the meal.

"What are you working on these days, Colinn?" I asked.

"Not much," he said, spearing a potato. "A couple of film scores. Maybe you can give me your opinion on them later. You too, Darren."

My cousin grimaced. "I'd be no use, Colinn. I'm tone deaf, remember? Music goes right past me."

"Which reminds me," Colinn said, returning his attention to me. "I have a new piano that you must try out. That is, if you don't mind…"

"A free concert, is it?"

He blushed. "Not at all, I only meant…"

"I know," I replied, raising a hand. "I'm just pulling your leg. I'd be happy to try it out. Playing for friends is much different from playing for an audience."

He relaxed. "Good. Busy schedule lately?"

"Insane," I said, laying down my knife and fork on the empty plate.

"Vienna one day, Dublin the next, Tallin, Lucerne, New York…But one must make a living."

"Come on, Roger," Darren said. "You know you enjoy it. You could play twenty-four hours a day."

"Not that much," I laughed.

"He was born in a piano," Darren said to Colinn in a mock aside.

Colinn brought Bramley apple pie and custard, and we finished our meal in a jovial mood. I sighed with inward relief that the subject of occultism hadn't come up. That said, I did detect a certain tension during the meal and the sensation that Colinn's good humor was somewhat forced.

Afterward, he took us into a nicely decorated living room, where a fire crackled in the fireplace. To my relief, I saw no overt signs of Colinn's dark interests. I'd imagined a house filled with crystal balls, pentagrams, and the odd human skull or two.

"Here she is," he said, indicating the ebony black concert grand that dominated the room. "My new pride and joy."

I opened the cover, sat down on the bench, and after a brief study of the score on the music stand, let my fingers roam over the silky-smooth keys.

"I'll never understand how you can do that," Colinn said. "Reducing an orchestral score to a piano version as you go."

I shrugged. "A gift, I suppose."

The music was typical Colinn: melodic, lush, with just enough of a bite in the harmonies to avoid sentimentality. And yet there was something else, something I'd never heard in his music before. I found it nearly impossible to describe; an impression of decadence, of depravity, as if something impure had infected his music.

But it wasn't merely the notes; it was the way they issued from the piano. It wasn't out of tune, not in the slightest. I have played many pianos in my life, but never encountered one with such an unusual tone. It was decidedly odd.

"What do you think?" Colinn asked when I finished.

"What sort of movie is it for?" I countered, not wishing to speak my mind. After all, my impressions could have been totally wrong; the product of stress and fatigue.

"A romantic comedy," he said.

I had an immediate vision of the type of low-budget film it would be. "I suspect it will suffice quite well," I said, and Colinn looked pleased.

I removed Colinn's score and from memory played several Bach fugues, Brahms' *Rhapsody in B minor*, and Liszt's *La Campanella*, feeling a cleansing sensation wash over my soul. The tone of the piano was perfectly delightful, even lovely.

"Where did you get this piano?" I asked, diving into Rachmaninoff's *Prelude in G minor* for a rousing conclusion.

"From the estate of the late Terrence Crowther," Colinn said from the depths of a vast armchair. "At a good price, too."

"Terrence Crowther?" I exclaimed, almost losing my place. "Wasn't he confined to an insane asylum?"

"He was a genius," replied Colinn defensively. "With eccentricities prone to being misinterpreted and misunderstood."

I shook my head. "Not from what I heard."

"Which was what?"

"That he threw away his millions on occult artifacts and mediums and the like. His family finally had him committed."

"Tabloid fantasies," Colinn said, in a tone that indicated he wanted no further discussion, and I let the subject drop.

Later, after we had retired to our rooms and Colinn was securing the house for the night, Darren came to me. "Who was this Crowther?" he asked.

"A minor composer of dubious ability and bizarre interests," I said. "He obtained something of a cult following. He was rumored to be involved in Satanic rituals and several followers even claimed that he was possessed."

Darren shivered. "Good thing it's only his piano that's here and not him."

"Colinn has always had a fascination that way, too," I said. "A decidedly unhealthy interest if you ask me."

Darren didn't reply. Instead, he took his leave.

Afterward, I fell asleep quickly, the gentle nocturnal noises of the countryside so much more conducive to rest than the clamor of the city.

It was in the pre-dawn hours that I was awakened by distant music. At first I thought I was dreaming, and it took me some minutes to realize that the sounds were coming from downstairs. I threw on my clothes and went to investigate.

Colinn was seated at the piano, still in his pajamas and wearing a dressing gown.

And the notes coming from his fingers…

The stairs creaked, and his gaze shot over to me. "Roger! Perfect timing! I've just added the finishing touches."

"At this time of the morning?"

"I always work better at night," he said. "The witching hour, you know."

"What is it?" I asked, finishing my descent. He motioned for me to join him on the piano bench so I slid in beside him.

"A sonata for four hands. Play it with me, won't you?"

For some reason, I hesitated. The notes that I had heard…

"What's the matter?" he asked.

"Nothing."

"It's really impractical to play a piece written for four hands with only two," he said with a wry smile.

I shouldn't have begun to play. I should have heeded the curious revulsion that rose up inside me; made an excuse of some sort…

As it was, I began to play with Colinn, who was an adequate although not exceptional pianist.

"You didn't compose this, did you?" I said before we'd finished even the first page of what was proving to be a fiendishly difficult piece that reminded me vaguely of Scriabin's *Black Mass* sonata.

"No," he admitted. "At least, not all of it."

"Who did?" I asked, although I felt that I already knew.

"Terrence Crowther," Colinn replied. "I found the manuscript tucked inside the piano. It was incomplete, and I've been laboring to finish it. But it's strange, though…"

"How so?"

"Whenever I sit down to work on it, I feel almost that it's not I who's writing it, but that the music just seems to come to me from outside; as if Crowther himself was writing through me."

The piano had taken on the same unusual tone that it had possessed before, as if it became a different instrument depending on the music being performed.

"This will be the first time the entire score has been played as it should be, with four hands," Colinn said as the music ventured far afield from the rather sinister melancholy with which it had begun.

"Is this why you invited me to come?" I asked, suddenly understanding.

"I hope you don't mind."

Colinn's fingers ranged along the lower keyboard, pounding out a driving rhythm that compelled me to increase the tempo. We sat there, side by side, shoulders hunched, hair flopping with the effort. Perspiration rolled off our foreheads and dripped onto the keys until they became slick and slippery. Inside the piano, the flying hammers struck the wires in a wild cacophony of sound until any semblance of musical normalcy was obliterated by the insane fury.

Then we entered eerie realms of twisted harmonies where strange, sinuous melodies slithered up and down the keyboard alternating with violent percussive outbursts, jagged leaps, and agonized intervals. The result was malevolent, evil…frighteningly so…and I felt as if my very soul was being ripped asunder. I wanted to stop but couldn't, the rhythm forcing me on against my will.

Suddenly—was it minutes or hours later?—I sensed that the wild music was approaching a terrible climax; one that I desperately wanted to avoid but couldn't. It was as if the piano itself had taken control of my hands. I desired to tear them away, but I was helpless in the grip of something more powerful than myself. I could no more remove my fingers from the ivory keys than if they had been glued there.

Although the first rays of daylight slanted into the room, they could not dispel the shadows that danced and played about on the surrounding walls, cast there by a fire that flickered in the grate. And as we played, the shadows grew, chased away the daylight, and a darkness like a living thing inched up the legs of the piano, lapped at the bench where Colinn and I sat, creeping towards us…

Then, at that very moment, the music reached its inevitable, damnable climax. The music that I wished with all my being would stop…and it did; or at least part of it did as Colinn's hands lifted from the keyboard.

As my own fingers continued to create nightmarish cascades of sound, Colinn turned to me.

"Thank, you, Roger!" he said ecstatically. "I knew I could count on your skill to carry on the piece by yourself."

The darkness surged forward and rose up past his legs, his waist, his chest…

"Colinn…!" I began hesitantly.

"Don't stop! Not now! Not when the incantation is nearly complete! I must welcome *Him*!"

I forced my eyes to focus on the complex score in front of me.

Suddenly, Colinn screamed, a shriek of pure terror. Whatever was happening was not what he'd expected. Then his scream became a gurgle, as if his throat were being crushed.

"Master!" he croaked, his voice now a whisper. "Why…?"

With all the will I could muster, I dragged my head around to look where Colinn was sitting. To this day I thank Providence that all I could see was darkness, but darkness in the shape of a man; a thing with Colinn's voice whose last sound was a death rattle…

And then the hideous, hungry darkness began to abate. It retreated from Colinn's body like melting wax and as I continued to play that hellish sonata, it began to lap around my own body, to climb higher and higher. I felt the breath congeal in my lungs and a scream form in my throat…

Then, like the crack of a gunshot, a door slammed upstairs. Startled, my hands jerked from the keyboard. With a final repellent discord the ghastly music ceased.

The darkness vanished, and drenched in sweat, I blinked in the bright morning sunshine that bathed the room.

Darren called in annoyance, "What's all the racket? Can't a man sleep in a little around here? It's flaming early, it is!"

I wobbled to my feet and leaned against the piano for support. I groped in my pocket for a handkerchief to wipe my forehead.

"What's the matter, Roger?" Darren asked. "You look like you've just seen a ghost."

"Worse than that," I whispered. "Much, much worse."

Darren descended a few steps to a curve in the staircase where he could see past the open lid of the piano. "What do you..." his voice scaled upwards into a shriek. "Is that Colinn?"

The color drained from his face, Darren rushed down the remaining steps into the living room. "He's dead!"

I forced myself to look.

Colinn—what remained of him—still sat there, hands poised above the keyboard as if ready to strike the next notes. But his face was frozen in a rictus of pure horror, his lifeless eyes staring, his entire body seeming no more than a shriveled husk, as if the life had been drained from it like a fly sucked empty by a spider.

"Yes," I said. "You'd best call the police."

"What...what happened?"

I held Darren's concerned gaze for a long moment. "Nothing that you or anyone else will believe," I replied, wondering what exactly the medical examiner would make of it.

Darren went for the phone.

I noticed that Baron was standing downcast by the door. "You can come with me, old boy," I said, rubbing his head. "I'll take care of you."

Darren returned. "They're on their way."

The room felt stuffy. I pushed open the French doors, and a gust of wind swirled past me and blew the accursed sheet music to the floor.

I went over to collect the pages.

A few embers still lingered in the fire. I shoved the score into them and blew until flames burst into life and devoured the paper.

"What was that?" Darren asked.

"Something that should never have been written," I said, as we exited the house to wait outside for the arrival of the authorities. "And which must never be played again."

five

RED MOLLY

Michigan, c. 1933

"Do you believe in ghosts?"

"Course not. Do you?"

"Think I might."

"Wimmin's stories, that's all."

The two men's voices come to me as I sit smoking my pipe and watching a weather-beaten freighter load up at Marquette's pocket ore dock. She's an ugly old ship, paint peeling and hull rusted so bad I can't even make out her name, and yet something within me wishes I was on board her.

I stretch out my legs to avert a cramp, and tell myself not to be a foolish old man.

Still, even though I can no longer be *at* sea, I can at least be *near* it, and hours spent at the harbor looking out over the endless, beautiful, treacherous expanse of Lake Superior go some ways in assuaging my sense of loss and uselessness. Especially on a nice day like this when the sun's warm and there's just enough of a breeze to keep from getting too hot.

"You sayin' I'm a girl?"

"No offense, mate. I just don't believe everything I hear in a saloon, that's all."

The men sit a little distance apart near the water's edge, but not far away enough to prevent me hearing their conversation over the chugging and rattling of the steam engines crossing the trestle to the top of the dock and the rumble of ore cascading down the chutes into the freighter's holds. They're obviously sailors—one's darning a faded jersey, the other whittling a piece of wood—and may or may not be familiar. When you've shipped with as many men as I have over the decades, faces—all but the most memorable of them—tend to run together. And there's nothing remotely memorable about these two.

Their discussion continues for a few minutes more without reaching a consensus, then one of them says, "Why don't we ask the Cap'n?"

I hadn't been aware that they'd noticed or recognized me, but obviously they had, as they both turn to look in my direction, before climbing to their feet and approaching.

"Beggin' your pardon, sir," says the taller, touching his cap, "it's Cap'n Porter, isn't it?"

"Aye," I say.

"Could you settle a disagreement between me and him?"

"Take a seat, boys," I say, indicating with my pipe the stone wall serving as my bench. "And you are...?"

"Nick," the one who'd spoken to me replies, perching on my portside. He looks to be about forty-five, with rumpled brown hair and a face that's stared into many a nighttime gale. "Nick Falson. This here's Rafe Lewis."

His companion, who plonks himself down starboard, is perhaps twenty. He's blond, stouter, with a crooked nose and lumpy ears.

"You've sailed with me?" I inquire.

Rafe shakes his head, but Nick agrees. "Years ago. On the *Preston Rose.*"

"I remember her well. She was a good ship."

And those were the good days when I was still fit and agile, before the sea and the weather and the hard grind had taken their toll.

"I overheard you talking," I say, "and 'tis an interesting subject you've chosen to disagree about. And I don't know as I can give you a firm answer one way or the other. But let me tell you a tale and you can decide. Did you ever hear of Red Molly?"

"A ship?" Rafe asks, while Nick says, "Never, sir."

I laugh. "You're too young, lads. Time was when every sailor in Marquette knew Red Molly. Really knew her, if you catch my drift."

"A whore?" Nick guesses, throwing a few more stitches into his jersey.

"She preferred to be called a sailor's friend." I puff on my pipe. "But after a few years she became real particular. Not for the likes of you. Only masters and owners for Red Molly."

"Why was she called Red?" Rafe asks, whetting his knife.

"Because she always wore a scarlet scarf around her neck," I explain. "Don't know why…but it marked her out from the other tarts hanging around the docks.

"Anyway, it was back in '83, and my story concerns Red Molly and Joshua Stanton. Joshua and I went way back. We'd grown up side by side, although he was a year or two older. We played together, sailed together, and loved the same girl. And let me tell you, Marybelle was the purtiest lass you ever saw. Many lads were lookin' at her, despite her old man bein' a judge, and a mighty tough one at that, but she only had eyes for one—and that was Joshua. He was tall, strong, good-looking in a rugged sort of way—just the type to turn the heads of all the girls when he'd walk down the street."

Rafe laughs. "We should be so lucky."

"They turn the other way when they see me coming," Nick laments.

"Back then," I add, "Joshua was as good as man as ever walked a deck. A bit of a temper, mind you, and once or twice I saw him really lose it, but what man doesn't?

"Well, Marybelle was always nice to me, but Joshua had caught her fancy. There was nothing I could do to make her change tack—and I tried mighty hard—so I had to settle for bein' best man at the weddin'."

"Tough luck," Nick commiserates.

"Tough wasn't it. I felt as though I'd been keelhauled. To lose your girl to your best friend…it's enough to tear the heart out of a man. Well," I say, "I tried to make the best of it, although I can't deny as how I didn't feel a twinge of jealousy every now and then when I'd see them walkin' arm in arm.

"Anyway, Joshua eventually becomes a captain, and a right good one. I was first mate, then, and was always glad to sail with him. He ran tight ships but mostly they were happy ones. And when he finally gets his own ship, well of course it has to be named the *Marybelle* after his wife. Fine topsail schooner, she was. Rugged little ship with nice lines."

I sigh. My pipe has died, and I tap out the ashes.

"But something went wrong. I don't know exactly what changed Joshua—he never confided in me—but something did. Maybe it was stress—I know there was a stillbirth—or money problems, or maybe something he inherited from his old man, who weren't no saint–"

"Or maybe it was something he caught," Nick interjects, looking up from his sewing, and I shoot him a sharp glance.

"You're gettin' ahead of my tale, lad," I say, shaking my empty pipe at him. "Whatever, Joshua goes from being clean and sober to drinking more than's good for him. His temper gets worse, and his ships…they aren't so happy any more.

"Neither's Marybelle. It broke my heart when sometimes I'd see her with a bruise on her face or her arm—although of course she tried to hide them behind a veil or by wearing long sleeves. When I'd ask her what had happened, she'd always tell me it was an accident of some sort. Maybe the first time or two I believed her, but after that…

"I offered to knock some sense into Joshua's head, 'cos my blood could boil from time to time, too, but she implored me not to. 'He'd only hurt you worse,' she says, and it's true, 'cos Joshua was a bigger man then me, and he knew how to use his fists.

"Well, word begins getting around that Joshua's keeping company with Red Molly—and had been, for some time. At first I don't credit it—who would want Red Molly when he has a girl like Marybelle at home? Not that Red Molly was bad looking, not at all—but would you rather sail on a trim schooner that's been well-kept or some weather-worn ship that's been sailed harder than was good for her? So one day I follow him to see for myself. And it's true. Him and Molly dancing together, kissin' and canoodlin', and then headin' upstairs to a room, his arm around her waist. I felt sick.

"I don't know how he fell in with her, or when, but there it was. Do I say anything to Marybelle? There's no need. I can see in her eyes that she knows the rumors are true. All I can do is give her a shoulder to cry on now and then. But it makes me burn inside, I can tell you that, and it's all I can do to be civil to Joshua.

"Time goes by and I end up shipping with another captain for a while, and it's a few months before I cast up at Marquette again. When I do, it's to find that things have gone from bad to worse. Marybelle's a shadow of her former self—all lean and skinny and 'fraid-looking like she'd seen one of the ghosts you boys was arguing about. And Joshua—he looks like a man bein' blown downwind to hell. And there's Red Molly on his arm, all gussied up and lookin' mighty pleased with herself. Folks say she's decided she wants Joshua all for herself—him being a successful captain with his own ship and all. Wants him to ditch Marybelle for her."

Rafe whistles. "And does he?"

"Well," I say, "on the other side's her daddy the judge. Big man in town. Could ruin Joshua for ever—put a word in the right ears and Joshua never gets a good cargo again. Plus there's the money that Joshua stands to inherit, Marybelle being an only child.

"Joshua's in a bind. 'Cos Red Molly's not about to let him go. She's stuck to him stronger than a barnacle on a piling. I heard she threatened to curse him if he ever tried to skip out on her—come back and haunt him, she would. Now here's the first strange thing. I take another voyage, and when I come back, Red Molly's gone!"

"Gone?" Nick echoes.

I snap my fingers. "Just like that. Vanished. I ask around, but no one seems to know what's happened to her. Some folks say she's left town, but that wouldn't have been like her—unless the judge had paid her to ply her trade elsewhere. Some say that Joshua's seen her off—hit her over the head with a belaying pin, put her in a barrel and sunk her somewhere she won't come up again."

Rafe scrapes off a piece of his whittling, while I reach in my pocket for my tobacco pouch and begin to refill my pipe.

"What did Cap'n Stanton say?" Nick asks.

"He didn't," I reply. "Kept his mouth shutter than a nailed-down coffin. I only had the guts to ask him once and he chewed me up one side and down the other. So Red Molly's gone. But Joshua—he's no better. Still loses his temper, still drinks—if anything, more than ever. I can't reason with the man—God knows I try. And Marybelle—maybe she ought to leave him, but she doesn't. I know there were fellas who would have loved to have taken up where Joshua left off—myself among them—but she'd never look at another man as long as he was alive. 'A vow's a vow,' she says. Never known anyone as loyal and as long-sufferin' as she was."

I tamp down the tobacco and light it. "I'd hear whispers in the saloons—men would say that that Marybelle would be better off if Joshua made a premature departure from this earth. It was all idle sailor-talk, mind you. But it tells you the esteem in which they held Marybelle that they'd even think of sending Joshua to his particular judgment a mite early."

"Which," I say, "brings me to my final voyage with Joshua, and the interesting part of my story."

Both men lean in a little closer.

"Joshua had a cargo to transport to Duluth, where he'd load up again, stop at Copper Harbor and then Sault Sainte Marie before returning to Marquette. It was getting towards the end of October, and you know what that means—winter's not far off. Indeed, you could feel it in the air. But Joshua wants to run one last cargo before the storms and the ice set in."

"But on the Lakes, you never know," Nick says, shivering. "They've swallowed many a good ship and many men."

"Darn right," I say. "And I wouldn't have gone, except Joshua asked me if I'd be his first mate, and I didn't like to say no. Did it for Marybelle too, of course."

"For Marybelle?" Rafe wonders.

"Yes," I reply. "Because Joshua, she tells me, is barely capable of being master of a vessel anymore. His mood changes faster than the weather— and worse, too. He complains constantly of headaches, has trouble concentrating, and sometimes he's confused. Every now and then he says that his vision isn't right. Then she discovers he's taking some kind of tincture of mercury."

"I was right!" Nick exclaims, slapping his thigh. "Red Molly gave him the pox!"

"Maybe," I reply. "Or maybe he was afraid of that curse. And so we sail from Marquette one clear day. Oh, there are a few clouds in the sky, and a nip in the air, but the breeze is fresh and soon the *Marybelle's* dancin' over the waves. Aye, 'tis a beautiful day. But Joshua's in one of his irascible moods. Nothing the men do is right. He's stomping around the deck cussin' and swearin'…giving orders, then changing his mind."

"I've sailed with captains like that," Nick says, spitting on the ground.

"Aye. Well I try to calm him down, but it's like trying to coddle a wolverine. Finally he goes below to have a tot of rum, and seems calmer when he returns.

"We're still sailing smoothly when the moon comes up and floods the lake with silver. At first it seems the night will be clear, but then a mist begins to arise. Joshua and I are standing together, studying the set of the sails. 'What's that?' I say, pointing to the topsail.

"Joshua peers upwards. 'Nothing,' he growls.

"'You sure?' I say.

"'Just mist in the shrouds,' he answers, giving me a puzzled look. "You never seen mist afore?"

"'Suppose so,' I reply, and he heads to his cabin, leaving me to mind the deck alone. The breeze drops in the middle of the night, leaving us becalmed, and the next day finds us drifting in thick fog. Joshua frets and fumes, but there's nothing to do but sit there and wait for the wind to pick up. Daylight's fading when finally a slight breeze comes, and the *Marybelle* gathers way.

"'Haul up those braces, you lazy sons!' Joshua shouts, and the crew—there's about a dozen—spring to work.

"'There it is again,' I say, indicating the mainmast rigging.

"Joshua squints, then regards me strangely. 'Something the matter with your eyes, Thomas?'

"'But don't you think it looks like—"

"'Like what?' he asks, and I lean over to whisper in his ear. He jerks back like he's been shot. 'Don't you ever say that again!' he exclaims. 'It's fog. Fog,' he repeats, but this time he doesn't sound too sure of himself.

"Come morning, the fog's thinned out and the wind's freshened, but not to our liking, and the waves are higher. 'Be in for a blow,' I say. 'Not yet,' Joshua replies, scenting the air. 'Hold her steady, Thomas.'

"Joshua stays below most of the day. When I go to report to him it's to find him taking a hearty draught of his medicine and washing it down with an even heartier dose of rum.

"'For the head, Thomas,' he says and indeed I think he doesn't look too shipshape. His face is drawn and his eyes are bleary and his hands are shaking. He even has to ask me what day it is and which port we're heading for.

"Finally the wind shifts, and the *Marybelle* begins to scud along. Not long after nightfall I find Joshua on deck staring into the night sky.

"'You sure there ain't somethin' there?' I ask, but he merely rubs his eyes, curses, and turns away.

"Well, the wind holds, and we make Duluth without incident, unload our cargo, and head back to sea, making for Copper Harbor. Joshua's none too steady—either on his pins or in his mind—and so it's up to me to get us out of the harbor and underway. Joshua had seemed out of sorts and occasionally confused before, but he's more so now. And nervous to boot. He roams the ship muttering under his breath, every now and then darting quick glances into the rigging."

Nick asks, "Normal, to look aloft, ain't it?"

I shake my head. "He wasn't studying the set of the sails, if that's what you mean. More as if...as if he was looking for something that shouldn't be

46

there. Like he was scared of something… or someone. And it wasn't just me that noticed. The men were becoming nervous as well. I see them exchanging dark looks and whispering to each other when they think none of the officers is listening."

I take a breath and release it slowly. "That first night out, the moon's bright, with clouds drifting across the sky. I'd been giving instructions to the second mate, for the watch was his, when Joshua lurches alongside. Just then a low cloud dims the moonlight, and in the sudden shadows, I grab his arm with one hand and point aloft with the other and say, 'Joshua, look!'

"His breath hisses in as he glances up. 'No, it can't be… not her…' he whispers. Then he spins around to face me. 'You're putting me on, Thomas! There's nothin' there, I tell you! Nothin'!' He digs his fingers into my shoulders for a moment, then turns and staggers away, one hand pressed to the side of his head. 'It can't be…it can't be…'

"The second mate's regarding me with anxiety in his eyes. 'Don't worry lad,' I say. 'You and I'll see the *Marybelle* through.' That seems to reassure him, but the sea's rough and so I keep watch through most of the night as well."

"It's the moon, ain't it?" Rafe says. "Does queer things to a man."

"I don't think it was the moon," I say. "Next day, Joshua's kind of quiet. Sits by himself a lot, pays no attention to the ship. But we know the weather's changing. The temperature drops, and ice forms on the rigging. But Joshua just sits there. I drape an oilskin around him so as he won't freeze. But it's as if he's waiting for something bad to happen. Comes nightfall, and it's pretty, with the moonlight shining off the ice and the stars bright.

"'What is it?' I ask, coming over to where Joshua's sitting and following his gaze. 'What's up there? Is it -'

"Suddenly he jumps to his feet, and his face is flushed and eyes wide. 'Go away!' he yells. 'Leave me alone!' At first I think he's talking to me, but he isn't.

"'You made me do it!' he cries. 'You wouldn't let me go!'

"'What's the matter with the cap'n?' asks the second mate, who's standin' nearby, but I just motion him away, put my arm around Joshua's shoulder, steer him below, and stow him in his bunk, where he lies shakin' and moanin' til mornin'.

"So we make Copper Harbor, to unload some crate and take on new cargo, but nobody's workin' real fast.

"'The men think there's something wrong on the *Marybelle*,' I explain to Joshua when he complains about them.

"'There ain't nothin' wrong!'

"'They're afraid that…maybe the ship's cursed—or haunted.'

"He goes pale for a moment, then makes a fist. 'Superstitious fools! What would give them that idea?'

"'They say that maybe it's something to do with you…'

"He smacks one hand into the other but I can tell that he's struggling for control and that it's more bluster than anything. 'Then let them say it to my face.'

"'*I'm* saying it to you, Joshua. You've not been yourself. Maybe your conscience—'

"'Conscience? What about my conscience?' he says so fiercely that I back away.

"'A man's conscience can do strange things to him,' I say, 'make him see things—'

"By now he's about as pale as a sheet. 'I should lay you out on the deck, I should,' he rasps, 'friend or not! I never saw anything until you—'

"He breaks off, then says in a hard tone, 'Get those lazy swabs to work. There's not time for this tomfoolery.'

"'Aye, Cap'n,' I say. We don't exchange more'n two words the rest of that whole day, which is just as well, since Joshua's downright jittery. Scared, I reckon.

"Come morning and there's snow in the air and the wind's blowin' from the nor'east.

"'We'd best stay where we are,' I say, but Joshua will have none of it. 'We're bound for the Soo, and we're going to make the Soo.'

"'But Joshua—it could get mighty bad out there—'

"'The *Marybelle's* handled worse. Go ashore yourself if you're not man enough to brave it.'

"I was tempted to stay ashore, but I'd promised Marybelle I'd take care of Joshua. And so we set sail. We're hardly clear of the harbor when we know that we're in for a real blow. The wind's howling a gale, and we have to reef the topsails. The spray's lashing over the bow, and we're rolling and tossing like a cork. A precious few miles we make, tryin' to claw ourselves away from land. And then things go from bad to worse. We hit a reef.

"The mainmast cracks in the middle and goes over the side. We're broadside to the waves which just pound us. The poor *Marybelle* takes on water right fast.

"'We've lost her,' I say, but Joshua doesn't answer, just stares into the tattered sails that the wind is ripping to shreds. 'We got to abandon ship!' I yell, trying to make myself heard over the howl of the wind and the crash of the breakers, but I might as well not exist.

"His face is white, and his eyes are wide. 'You've ruined me!' he hollers, up to where the clouds and spray are whipping through the rigging so hard that you can't tell one from another. 'What more do you want?'

"The second mate's tugging on my sleeve. 'The yawl, sir,' he says.

"I know he's right. The *Marybelle* can't last more than a few minutes. If we want a chance to survive——because land's not far off—we have to go.

"'Joshua!' I shout. 'Come along!' I try to grab him, but he shoves me away. 'Are you blind?' he cries. 'It's her!'

The *Marybelle's* being beaten to splinters. The deck's heaving with every wave, and planks are cracking like gunshots.

"'You've got my ship!' he screams, 'Isn't that enough? Go away! Go away!'

"'Sir!' the second mate pleads. 'It's no use.'

"I try one more time. 'Joshua!' but he's shaking his fist towards what's left of the mast. 'You fiend!' he shrieks as another wave froths across the deck, nearly sweeping me off my feet.

"'We're going, with or without you,' the second mate says to me. I think about tryin' to manhandle Joshua, but know it would be no use. So I turn to go with the mate.

"Somehow we manage to launch the yawl in the lee of the *Marybelle* and cast off. The wind drives us towards the shore. And the last we see of

Joshua, he's still standing on the deck as the *Marybelle* breaks up around him."

I pause.

Nick and Rafe are regarding me curiously.

"By some miracle we all make it safely to land," I say, "and fortunately there's a cottage nearby because we're nearly dead from cold. A fire never felt so good. Next day, when the storm's blown over there's little left of the poor *Marybelle* but her ribs sticking out from the reef like the carcass of a beached whale."

"And Cap'n Stanton?" Nick asks quietly.

"His body washes up the next day," I say. "They call me to identify him. And here's the strangest thing of all—knocked me on my beam ends when I saw it. Clutched in his hand is a scarlet scarf, just like Red Molly used to wear."

We sit in silence for a moment, looking out over the waters of the lake.

Rafe taps a foot on the ground. "Blowed if I can make heads or tails of it."

"As I said, I can't give you a firm answer," I finish.

Then there's a soft touch on my shoulder.

"It's time for supper, dear," says a warm voice.

I turn around and meet my wife's smile.

"Must go, boys," I say, climbing to my feet.

And hand in hand, Marybelle and I walk home.

six

HOUNDED BY NIGHT

This is not the way it's supposed to be. Why can't I get it right? Why can't I stop them? They are still after me. I know it. I feel it...

Officer Steffan Rogers of the Muskrat Mountain Police Department studied the several sheets of crumpled yellow legal paper he held in his hand. They fluttered in the light spring breeze, making the angular, tormented script in which they were written seem even more agitated.

"I found them on the table beside his bed," said the middle-aged woman wearing a floral print dress and cardigan standing on the other side of the chain-link fence. She'd been loitering outside when he pulled his squad car into the driveway of the white-painted colonial style house, and had promptly called out to him the moment he stepped out of the car. He'd figured he might as well get the interview with the neighbor out of the way first. She turned out to be a past-her-prime dog-fancier who was as artificially groomed as the trio of bowed and scented Westies that romped in her immaculate yard.

"Why did you pick them up?" Steffan asked. "Don't you know that's tampering with evidence?"

"I wanted to make certain you saw them, officer," the woman replied. Her name was Mrs. Esmerelda Tiefenthaler. Steffan mentally referred to her as 'ET'. "I didn't mean to do anything wrong," she continued. "But you hear stories of the police overlooking something obvious…although I'm sure *you* never would…"

"What else did you touch?" he asked sternly.

"Why…nothing!" she exclaimed, flustered. "I walked through the house to make sure Paul—Mr. Groundstone—wasn't lying on the floor dead or something. You know what middle-aged men are like. My Harold died that way. Just dropped like a stone while brushing his teeth. Heart, you know…" She pressed a hand to her more-than-ample bosom and mimicked a grimace.

Steffan sighed, thinking to himself that perhaps the late Harold had been lucky. "Did you know the missing man well?"

She nodded vigorously. "Paul—that is, Mr. Groundstone—and I have been neighbors for years."

"And competitors?"

"Of course." She indicated a badge sewn onto the front of the turquoise cardigan. MMKC. Muskrat Mountain Kennel Club. "My Bitsy took best in show last May."

"And how did you learn he was missing?"

"It was Patches." She smiled at a long-bodied, grayish-blue dog lying on the grass by her feet. It made eye contact with Steffan, emitted a low growl, and bared its teeth. Steffan ignored it. Show dogs—conformation, to be technical—were not the same as obedience or agility dogs. He'd watched dog shows on TV. All conformation dogs had to do was be led around the ring on a leash and stand for an exam. What mattered was how they measured up to breed standard, not what their manners were like, particularly out of the ring. Many were sadly lacking.

"Patches, hush!" ET admonished. "I heard Patches barking in the house when I let out my own dogs. Paul was always outside with Patches precisely at 7:30. When I heard Patches barking and Paul didn't appear, I knew something must be wrong. So I went over. The door was locked, but there was no sign of Paul—Mr. Groundstone."

"How did you get in?"

She blushed. "I have a key. I watch the house when Paul's away."

"Did you notice anything unusual? Strange noises in the night?"

She shook her head. "Why, no, officer."

Steffan suppressed a yawn. At first, he'd been excited when the call had come in about the disappearance of a prominent citizen—the president of the local dog club. It was better than pulling over tourists speeding through Muskrat Mountain's antique- and bookstore-lined main street.

His interest had waned when a fellow officer—who had her finger on the pulse of the town's society doings—informed him that the widowed Groundstone's reputation extended beyond pampered pups, if he took her meaning. He did. Chances were, Groundstone had run off with someone he'd met in a dog show. He'd undoubtedly return from a rendezvous at a motel in a neighboring town…far enough from Muskrat Mountain to avoid being recognized.

"He didn't tell you he was leaving?" Steffan asked.

"Oh, no. And he'd never go without Patches." ET beamed at the dog, who obliged Steffan with another snarl when his glance instinctively fell on the dog again. "She's a champion. A Cardigan Corgi, you know."

He didn't know. Nor did he want to. These little yapping things didn't count as dogs in his book. He had a German Shepherd K9 named Gage in the back seat of his car. A real dog. The best partner he'd ever had. He didn't care for dogs that couldn't do anything but look prissy.

"These all of the papers?" he asked, holding them up.

She nodded. "I hope they help you find him. It won't be the same around here without Paul. Come, children," she said, beckoning to the dogs.

"One more question if you please," Steffan said, halting her. "Had you noticed any change in Mr. Groundstone's behavior lately?"

She paused and frowned. "Funny you should ask that, officer. He's seemed more distracted—and nervous—than usual over the past few weeks. Ever since…well, since he returned from China. Or was it Tibet?"

"Or Nepal?" Steffan asked with more than a hint of sarcasm.

ET didn't catch it. "They're all the same, really, aren't they?" she beamed.

Not to the inhabitants, Steffan thought, but didn't say. Instead, he asked, "Did something happen there?"

"I'm sure I don't know…wait a moment. He brought back a souvenir—a statue of a dog. The weirdest thing I've ever seen. When I asked him about it, he just muttered that he'd found it in a ruined temple on the Plateau of Long, or Leng, wherever *that* is—and changed the subject."

Steffan filed the information away. Was Groundstone guilty of stealing an item of cultural significance? Troubled by a twinge of conscience?

"Is there anything else?"

"And at dog shows…oh, I'm sure it doesn't matter…"

"Tell me," Steffan encouraged.

"Paul judged obedience as well as conformation," she said. "Dog owners have to put their dogs through certain patterns…quite simple really, left turn, right turn, about face…"

"Yes, I know that."

"Well, Paul was changing the patterns. Totally non-standard. Quite odd patterns, actually. Really sharp and angular."

"Why would he do that?"

"I have no idea," she said simply. "And he'd mumble while doing them—most judges don't speak except to issue commands."

"What did he mumble?" Steffan asked, feeling as if he was pulling teeth to get information.

She shrugged. "I only heard him once, and I couldn't make it out. It was like a formula or incantation perhaps…in Latin, or Arabic, or something like that. Pretty silly, right?"

Steffan thought that Latin and Arabic were quite dissimilar. Neither of course, were spoken around the Himalayas. Not that it was likely to be important.

"Thanks for your help," he said.

"No trouble," ET replied. She headed toward her house, the dogs following her obediently. "I left the door unlocked for you," she called back cheerfully over her shoulder.

Steffan rubbed his forehead, and decided to read further. Perhaps Groundstone's notes would give a clue as to his mental status—or his disappearance.

My first dream was on a Saturday. I had gone to bed late after judging a show in Great Point...my first attempt. It had been a long, hot day and I was tired. I ate only a light dinner, so my digestion wasn't to blame. I had trouble falling asleep. Eventually I must have done so.

The first thing I remember was the smell of dog urine—at least I supposed it to be so. The odor was acrid, but there was something odd about it, something unclean. And then I was...where? I cannot describe it, except that it was a large, open area. Around me dark, indefinable shapes moved in unusual, unnatural ways. And a sort of eerie keening or howling rose and fell in weird intervals and set my nerves on edge.

I thought I was invisible, in the dream, but then one of the shapes turned toward me...

And then I awoke with a headache and a sick feeling in the pit of my stomach.

Perhaps it was no more than a side effect of the Liao...

Steffan puffed out his cheeks. A bad dream. Of what help was that? He had bad dreams after work, too. He might today, if he couldn't find more to go on than a man who'd left home without taking his dog out to pee.

And what was Liao? Probably a drug of some sort that he'd never heard of. He could look it up later.

Perhaps he'd learn more from the house—the scene of the crime, if crime there had been. He crossed to the front door and pushed it open.

Paul Groundstone had money. Lots of it. The foyer was tiled in marble and guarded by a bronze statue of some female Hindu-appearing deity. An antique grandfather clock ticked in the corner of the wood-floored living room, keeping watch over a concert-sized grand piano—a Fazioli, Steffan noticed appreciatively, playing a quick scale on the silky-smooth keys. The elegant living room furniture looked French (Louis Quatorze, perhaps?) and was symmetrically arranged on a finely-woven Persian rug. Statuettes of corgis romped on the mantlepiece above the imposing brick fireplace. Expensive, yes, but also, he thought, somewhat incongruous. The living room of a wealthy man who lacked a woman's eye for domestic harmony.

He peeked into the dining room where a crystal chandelier hung above an oak table. A glass-fronted cupboard contained a collection of English teacups and saucers. Photos of corgis lined the walls.

A small but well-equipped gym caught his attention briefly, and he recalled that the other officer had also told him that Groundstone was a fitness buff. Ran marathons when he wasn't showing or judging dogs. Or seducing women. Or any two of the three together…

The bedroom—Groundstone apparently preferred to live on the ground floor—contained a queen-sized bed. The sheets were straight and a pair of pajamas was laid out ready for use. On the bedside table lay a collection of earplugs and a legal-sized notepad, presumably the one on which the papers he held had been written. A straight-backed chair beside the table faced a dresser with a television set across the room. Something struck him as strange about the room, but he couldn't place what.

The next room was obviously Groundstone's study. A pair of display cases overflowed with ribbons, certificates, trophies, and photos of show rings, several featuring the missing man. Piles of papers were neatly stacked on either side of the computer centered on a mahogany desk. He glanced at the topmost sheets—all had to do with dog club matters.

A rank of bookshelves dominated one wall. What did the president of the dog club read? Books on dogs…shelf after shelf of them. All but one. Perhaps Groundstone needed the occasional change of pace, but the row of books didn't fit the mental picture he'd been building of Paul Groundstone. The shelf sagged with the weight of volumes on the paranormal, the occult…mostly old volumes with tongue-twisting Latin titles that Steffan didn't attempt to pronounce, his only knowledge of Latin being a few stray phrases that crept occasionally into Mass. Several books included "UFO" in the title, and others appeared to be fiction. Steffan ran a finger along the spines: H. P. Lovecraft, August Derleth, Frank Belknap Long. He wasn't familiar with any of them.

He turned back to the desk.

One book, its title worn off a cracking leather binding, lay open, face down. He turned it over. The left hand page was written in English, while the right hand was in a flowing script that he didn't recognize.

"I stood on the pale grey shores beyond time and space," went the text. "In an awful light that was not light, in a silence that shrieked, I saw them…They are lean and athirst…all the evil in the universe is concentrated in their lean hungry bodies…"

Steffan snorted and flipped the page.

"There is an abyss of being which man has never fathomed…," it continued. "There is curved time and angular time. The beings that inhabit angular time cannot enter curved time…"

Steffan grimaced and laid the book down again. Definitely not his taste in fiction.

It was then he noticed the statue—surely the one to which ET had referred. He lifted it up. Made of some type of black stone, it was about six inches tall. It was, he supposed, a canine, although a breed he didn't recognize, being oddly distorted, as if its subject had been a warped, deformed specimen of its kind. But it was the markings that were most peculiar. Incised into the stone were curious, angulated patterns that seemed to have no relevance to the characteristics of a dog…not meant to represent fur or whiskers or whatever. No, they scrolled around the figure as if possessed of some arcane meaning…something ancient, born out of the intelligence of a long-lost race.

Steffan's skin crawled. He dealt with evil in its ordinary forms every day—murder, theft, rape, assault…He was no stranger to the dark side of human existence. Things by themselves weren't evil; people—and their actions—were. And yet this object struck him as if it contained a darkness of its own. Why had Groundstone felt compelled to appropriate it from the old temple?

He shook his head. He was being fanciful.

Possibly, though, the statue could be a clue. On impulse, he slipped it into his pocket.

Evidence. But evidence of what?

He continued his inspection of the house. The two-car garage contained a late model BMW sedan and a Mercedes convertible. Wherever Groundstone had gone, he hadn't driven there.

He went back outside and decided he might as well finish reading Groundstone's last known words. It was either that or return to the office and start filing a report. A report with very little to go on. The captain would really love that. He followed a path of paving stones and sat down on a bench shaded by a crabapple tree in full bloom.

It was about two weeks later when I dreamed again. Once more, there was the smell as of dog urine, but this time stronger. And the area seemed larger, and bounded with an irregular border that might have been mountains, but which rippled or vibrated. The light was hazy, with a greenish hue, and once again the weird howling filled the air. There was a sea that was like no sea on Earth, and angles and planes that made no sense.

Dark shapes crawled among those angles. And I knew somehow that they had seen me, scented me, wanted me...

I was their prey.

I could sense their ravenous, insatiable hunger, and their unquenchable thirst...and yet, they had no conception of hate or any other emotion familiar to human beings...

So I ran. I ran among the angles searching vainly for a curve. But before I could find one, I awoke drenched in sweat and shivering. My neck, legs, and back ached. I called the office and told them I was coming down with a virus and couldn't make it in to work.

Still no hint as to why Paul Groundstone had vanished. Steffan was beginning to doubt that he'd locate any useful information. Psychoanalysis wasn't his forte. He didn't want to waste his afternoon reading about Paul Groundstone's dreams.

Suddenly, he realized what was strange about the bedroom—there was no pen near the legal pad. Maybe it had fallen off and rolled under the bed. Maybe ET had 'borrowed' it.

One dream I could dismiss as a fluke; but two?

They're after me. That's the only logical conclusion. I need to find a way to control them before they find me here in this dimension. I feel certain that I can complete the patterns, recreate the planes needed to put them off the track using the dogs at the shows. But I need more time!

I have experienced nothing in the daytime, so if I can find some way to avoid dreaming, perhaps I can hold them off long enough…

I tried taking a nightcap to dull my senses. At first it seemed to work, and I slept peacefully for several days.

Nightcaps. And probably several martinis during the day, Steffan surmised. Not to mention the Liao.

A week passed, then two, then three, and I began to hope that I'd thrown them off the scent. But I was wrong. I dreamed again and found myself once more in that weird place composed of strange angles and teeming with formless shapes that filled me with dread.

And they were after me again—the Hounds of Tindalos, the priest had called them, though they weren't hounds or anything like Earthly canines at all. They were relentless, picking up my trail and pursuing me down the byways and alleys of space and time. I had violated their temple, glimpsed them when the priests had bowed themselves out of the room before they could see the things they worshiped. But I had seen what human eyes were never meant to see.

And now they are after me.

I can feel them. Sense them.

I can even hear their breathing.

And no matter what I do, they're never far behind.

I want to scream, to vent my frustration, to shout at them to leave me alone; but it would be hopeless. It might even bring them to me faster.

Steffan shuffled the pages. Only a couple more to go. Might as well finish. The man read weird fiction. He had weird dreams. No surprise there.

I began to use sleeping pills—over the counter, at first, and when I found that those didn't work, prescription ones. I tried to put myself into as deep a sleep as possible. I hoped that if I were drugged enough, I wouldn't be able to dream. It didn't work.

As bad as the previous dreams had been, the one last night was the worst. It came, once again, after a lapse of some three weeks. Three weeks in which I dreaded the coming of night, anxiety gnawing at me like a weevil chewing its way through a cotton boll, relentlessly, inexorably until it reaches the heart. Oh, how I long to avoid night, but how can I, when I have to be awake in the day to work with the dogs to find that cursed pattern?

And even if I tried to sleep in the day and stayed awake at night, would it really matter? Why should whatever is hunting me stop with daylight? Just because it hasn't so far…

Psycho. The man was psycho. He needed a good shrink. Steffan sighed and read on.

I can hardly bear to put down on paper what happened last night. I dreamed that I was again making my way through a landscape of strange, otherworldly angles. The fetid odor was almost overwhelming, the stench of decay nearly unbearable. The sickly yellow-green lighting made me imagine that I walked through a miasma rising from some ghastly swamp, yet the ground was firm underfoot.

Then the howling began. It assaulted my ears until the blood pulsed in my brain. Whatever was pursuing me was closer than ever. But the dream went on and my pursuer never caught up to me. Was it toying with me? Feeding on my fear? I ran and ran seemingly forever among the twisting, turning angles and planes, seeking a curve or avenue of escape that didn't exist.

And the breathing—the panting—drew nearer and nearer until I could feel warm breath gusting on the back of my neck…

Unable to restrain myself, I screamed my way down labyrinths of time until once again I found myself in the safety of a sane world, covered with sweat and goosebumps.

Steffan shook his head. It was crazy stuff, and yet he felt a twinge of pity for Groundstone; the man was obviously torn up over something.

Maybe the dog show judge was afraid that he himself was losing control, and expressed this in his dreams of being pursued by the very dogs he controlled at shows, now transformed into preternatural monsters.

Steffan turned the page. The handwriting had become shaky, the ink smeared and blotted.

I have attempted it once more. I've tried again to keep them away, but have I done it correctly? Is there even a correct way of doing it? There must be—because I cannot face the dreams again. I cannot allow myself to go to sleep. Whatever happens, I must stay awake. If I believed in God, I'd pray, but would He even listen to me?

It's 2 a.m. I don't know how much longer I can keep my eyes open, but if I close them, they'll be there, waiting for me, beyond the wall of sleep.

Breathing! I hear breathing!

But I'm not asleep! I'm not!

I must be hearing things.

Run. I must run...

That was it. Nothing more. Steffan folded the papers, put them in his pocket, and rose to his feet. One final thing to do. He walked around the exterior of the house, checking the windows for signs of forced entry. Not that he expected to find anything. There was no suspect, just a man who'd gone insane and most likely wandered off. Put out a missing persons report, and wait for someone to spot Groundstone.

His mind distracted, he almost missed it.

He passed behind the house, beneath the bedroom window, where a lilac bush was perfuming the air. Something glittering on the ground caught his attention, and he bent over to pick up a gold pen. And faintly in the grass, almost invisible, were footprints, heading, it appeared, toward the edge of the property.

He whistled to himself, then returned to the patrol car and released the rear door. Gage bounded out, ears and tail erect. Black, with golden-brown legs and chest, he looked every inch the police dog.

Steffan motioned with his hand. "This way, boy."

The big dog trotted beside him. They rounded the house to where

Steffan had found the pen and where faint footprints led away from the house. Steffan clipped on Gage's tracking harness, then retrieved the pen and held it to the dog's nose.

"Seek, Gage. Seek."

Gage sniffed the pen, then the ground, then trotted in the direction the tracks had taken. Behind the screen of trees at the boundary of the yard, an old lane, hardly more than a pair of rutted tracks, threaded through rolling, tree-dotted pastureland. Groundstone's footprints rapidly became invisible to Steffan, but Gage was full of confidence.

The trail wound between a pair of low hills, and then entered a patch of woodland. Here, the dog's pace slowed. There must be, Steffan surmised, a surfeit of other smells—rabbits, squirrels, perhaps fox or coyote.

"Seek," he repeated. "Keep to the trail, Gage."

The German Shepherd responded with a burst of concentrated effort. Steffan had to run to keep up, dodging and weaving between the trees.

They surged into an overgrown clearing, and Gage slammed to a stop, Steffan skidding to a halt behind him. The dog's hackles raised, and even Steffan felt a tingling at the back of his neck. Instinctively, he fell to his haunches beside the dog.

"What is it, boy?" he whispered.

Gage responded with a low growl and a fixed stare into the distance.

Steffan parted the brush to reveal an old church building, crumbling, overgrown, roof and walls sagging. Its windows were boarded up and paint peeled from the clapboards. A rusty bell still hung from a precariously canting belltower.

Steffan took a moment to reorient himself. Old St. Francis' Church. That must be it. Abandoned and deconsecrated some twenty years ago.

If Groundstone had wanted to pray, why would he have come here? There were several churches including an active parish with its own priest right in town. Had he come here because it was close to home, perhaps not realizing it had been closed?

Slowly, Steffan straightened. He unclipped Gage's tracking harness and let it fall to the ground. He wanted the dog loose.

"Let's check it out, boy."

Hackles still raised, Gage approached the building one step at a time. That wasn't like him. Gage normally raced like a bullet to take down a fleeing perp. There was nothing that gave the dog greater pleasure.

Steffan dropped his hand to his belt, slipped his 9mm Glock from its holster, and flicked off the safety.

The church's door hung open. Motioning to gage to halt, Steffan stood to the side of the door and listened.

Nothing.

He made a quick pointing movement with his finger and Gage shot through the opening. Steffan swung in behind him, dropping to a crouch with his gun raised.

Gage whined from the far corner.

In the light coming through the doorway, Steffan saw the dog nosing a crumpled figure lying against the far wall. He shoved the gun back into the holster and crossed over. Gage backed up and lowered himself into a sit.

"Don't!" the shattered wreck of a man moaned, raising shaking hands to a face smeared red from a bone-deep gash. "Leave me alone! *Leave me alone!*"

"Paul Groundstone?" Steffan asked. "I'm Officer Rogers of the Muskrat Mountain Police."

The man twitched and his eyes opened. Steffan flinched at the expression the bloodshot orbs held—it was the look of someone who had stared into the face of unimaginable horror and managed to turn away just before losing his reason.

Groundstone licked his lips. "Go away," he pleaded. "Get out of here. They'll be back. They'll get you too if you see them."

"Who will?" Steffan asked.

"I should never have hidden in that temple," Groundstone whined. "Never have tried to get a look at them when—when they were summoned. The priests warned me, but I wouldn't listen."

"What priests? Warned you about what?"

Groundstone seemed not have heard him. His haunted gaze darted around the room.

"What are you looking for?" Steffan asked, glancing around himself.

Groundstone's voice was a hoarse whisper. "*The Hounds.*"

"Hounds? What hounds?" Steffan shook Groundstone's shoulders. "We're not at a dog show, man."

"The Hounds of Tindalos," Groundstone replied with a shiver. "It's my fault they're here. I thought I'd discovered a new breed of dog, but I was wrong. I thought perhaps the tales were mistaken…exaggerated… designed to keep the curious away…and I wanted to see them, obtain one …and I saw what I should never have seen…"

He took a rasping breath. "Now they're here and I can't stop them. They're after me. I tried to ward them off but I couldn't get the patterns right."

"Patterns?" Steffan echoed. "Such as at the dog shows?"

Groundstone nodded jerkily. "Dogs can sense things humans can't…I thought that if I started them in a certain direction, they would instinctively find the proper patterns. I hoped they'd have something in common with the Hounds, but they don't…they have nothing in common. *Nothing!*" He touched the wound on his forehead.

Steffan reached into his pocket for a clean handkerchief to wipe the blood from Groundstone's face, but as he pulled it out, the dog statuette he'd taken from the house clattered to the floor.

Groundstone recoiled. "Get that thing away from me!" he shrieked, attempting to scrabble away, his foot sending the statuette spinning. "They'll sense that it's here! I should never have taken the hellish thing!"

"Pull yourself together, man!" Steffan urged. "Let me help you."

"Go away!" Groundstone insisted, his voice rising to a high-pitched wail. "If you value your life, get out of here!"

"Not without you," Steffan said. "Come one, I'll give you a hand." He gripped Groundstone's elbow.

Without warning, the building shuddered as if struck by a gust of wind. Dust trickled from the rafters. The weather-beaten door banged shut, wedging itself into the doorframe and plunging the interior into darkness. A single shaft of light penetrated through the dilapidated roof. The temperature plummeted.

For a moment, there was a deep, unnatural silence.

Then, from everywhere and nowhere the sound of breathing filled the air. Steffan glanced at Gage. *It wasn't coming from the dog.*

"Too late," Groundstone whimpered. "It's too late. They're here!"

Steffan started as Gage growled. The dog had gained his feet and was staring into the near corner of the building.

"*Stay,*" Steffan commanded him.

At first, Steffan saw nothing. Then a stream of black smoke—narrow at first, then widening—began to pour in from the angle of the wall, although there was no break in the boards.

His skin crawling and chest suddenly tight, Steffan rose and stepped back.

The smoke roiled and twisted, and in it, something moved.

Groundstone moaned in terror.

And then it appeared, materializing through the smoke, loping like a thing out of time into the present. It was formless, and yet its very formlessness reminded Steffan briefly of something vaguely wolflike. The instant passed and he knew that whatever it was, it didn't belong on Earth or anywhere else in a sane universe.

It was lean and powerful, a rippling darkness out of the unknown eons of Earth's forgotten past…something evil, obscene, misbegotten. And it stank, exuding a raw reek like dog urine coupled with the vile sweetness of decay. Steffan gagged as the putrid tide washed over him, graying his vision and enveloping him in a wave of dizziness that threatened to hurl him into unconsciousness.

His body froze even as his mind struggled to make sense of the shifting apparition. But it couldn't. There was nothing for it to fix on, only tortured distortion and dimensions beyond human perception. He thought he glimpsed glowing green eyes and slavering fangs and a tongue that dripped blue ichor…

The green eyes met his, and Steffan wanted to scream, run, *anything* to get away…but he couldn't.

For the eyes were cold, utterly expressionless…The eyes of a creature without pity, without conscience, without a hint of compassion. Only

65

insatiable hunger and unquenchable thirst.

The rippling darkness turned aside to enfold the quivering Groundstone in an obscene embrace. Its tongue lapped Groundstone's face in a vile parody of a dog's lick. The man's moans turned into sobs, then crescendoed into a piercing screech of absolute despair as the last strands of his sanity snapped. The sound hung in the air as if time had lost its meaning, then Groundstone himself appeared to shrink, collapsing in upon himself like a deflated balloon.

Steffan's subconscious must have blotted out the rest, because when he came to himself a moment later, Groundstone's agony was over. Then he sensed the thing's attention shift toward him.

The creature—the *Hound*—raised its formless head, and again Steffan glimpsed pitiless green eyes shining with an alien hunger.

His mind screamed at him to move. But he couldn't.

He felt his very essence being drawn toward the writhing vortex and knew that death—a ghastly, unimaginably horrible death—was only seconds away. He could almost feel the icy touch of darkness, when out of the shadows a black and tan streak flung itself into the smoke, ripping and clawing at the formlessness.

"Gage, no!" The words burst—too late—from Steffan's throat.

The creature bayed—an unearthly sound that no terrestrial throat could utter. Then it flung the dog away. Gage hit the wall with a thud and slid limply to the ground.

The spell broken, Steffan yanked out his sidearm and sent shot after shot into the shifting darkness. But what was he shooting at? There was nothing on which to draw a bead, only confusing angles and distorted planes.

The writhing darkness surged toward him. He stumbled away, but his heel caught on a nail protruding from a warped floorboard and he pitched onto his back, still firing as he fell. The Hound writhed over him.

He was going to die...

The thing's tongue—a hollow proboscis—extended toward him.

There was no escape. He had mere seconds left.

Steffan formed the sign of the cross on his chest with his free hand.

Then something growled, a low, menacing growl. Steffan glanced to his left.

It was Gage, bloodied, but with his ears erect, his gaze focused on the creature. He was crouching for another well-intentioned but hopeless spring, his eyes shining with the fierce dedication and determination that only a dog prepared to give his life for his master could have.

Steffan's mind raced.

In his dreams, Groundstone had been trying to escape the angles and planes and find a curve. And the book—*"they emerged from strange angles…the beings that exist in angular time cannot enter curved time…"*

Take away the angles…

It was a desperate idea. But it was all he could think of, since bullets were having no effect on the thing.

"Gage!" Steffan yelled, forcing out the words. "Circle it, Gage, circle it!"

He accompanied the command with a sweeping movement of his arm to indicate what he wanted the dog to do. The German Shepherd hesitated, uncertain.

"Circle," Steffan repeated, duplicating his arm motion.

Gage bounded forward, and continued around the writhing smoke.

"Again, boy!"

Gage circled around again, and needed no more instruction from Steffan to continue.

The thing—the *Hound*—halted. The swirling smoke weaved back and forth, and the creature inside it became even more nebulous, as if it was confused or blinded, as if Gage's actions were obscuring the angles, denying it a clear path to follow.

"Keep going, Gage!" Steffan called. Would the thing give up, go away? Perhaps, if he could get out of the building, the thing couldn't follow him. Steffan squirmed backwards; he didn't have much time—Gage couldn't circle the creature forever.

Something dug into his hip. Steffan groped with his left hand and found the dog statuette.

"Do you want this?" he shouted. "Take it!"

He hurled it at the Hound.

It sailed wide, and with a crack struck the old, dust-covered stone altar and shattered.

Again the creature howled, a howl that went on forever, that plunged into the abyss of time and echoed through the narrow angles of infinity.

And instead of falling to the ground, the pieces of the statue remained suspended in air for a long moment, defying gravity. Then the darkness that was the Hound swirled out to them, and pulled the fragments into itself.

And then the Hound drew back.

Starting from the rear it began to dissolve into smoke, a foul black stream that flowed into the corner whence it had come. Inch by dreadful inch it dissolved, as if being sucked into a vacuum…into nothingness. The last wispy threads of smoke rushed into the angle and vanished, and all that remained of the apparition was the lingering dog-like odor.

For a long moment, Steffan remained where he was, too dazed even to think. Gage, panting, collapsed beside him.

Steffan put his arms around the dog's neck and hugged him. "You did it, boy, you did it."

Gage's brown eyes seemed to say, *We took care of* him, *didn't we?* He got to his paws and shook, the tags on his collar jingling against his K9 officer's badge.

Remembering the gun in his right hand, Steffan reholstered the weapon and released Gage. He gained his knees, and ran his hands over Gage's body and legs. "You OK, buddy? Nothing broken?"

Jagged, bloody wounds coursed along the dog's flank. His right elbow was swollen. Otherwise, he seemed to be all right.

"I think you're going to make it," Steffan said, his legs wobbly as he stood up. "Groundstone's beyond help, though."

Grimly, he studied the shredded remains of what had once been Paul Groundstone, the body parts dripping with a strange blue ichor.

Steffan shivered. How was he going to write a report about this? Perhaps it would be best to say nothing. He'd found the missing man. Let the forensic pathologists determine the cause of death and try to explain the inexplicable.

He turned and led Gage out of the crumbling building, back into the sunshine and the fresh air.

"Be glad you're a dog," he said to his partner. "At least you're not tempted to open doors that have no business being opened."

He motioned. "Let's go home, Gage."

The peaceful woods enclosed them. But Paul Groundstone's last terrified scream still echoed in his ears, and Steffan dared not imagine what the man's being—his soul, for surely that was what the Hound had devoured—was enduring somewhere, in the dreadful recesses of the chaos that existed before the world was born.

A whisper like a faint breeze-

Steffan whirled, his hand reflexively going for the gun he knew would be useless.

It was only Gage, trotting happily behind him.

He repeated the words to himself as he cast a final look back at the church which both was and was no longer a church, containing the body of a man who both was and was no longer a man.

It was only Gage...

He took a deep breath.

Only Gage...

seven

DIES IRAE

Being a sequel to "Princess of Darkness" by Frederick Cowles.

It was with shock and distress that I learned of the death of my friend and former colleague in the Diplomatic Service, Harvey Gorton, in November of 1939 while resident at the Eastdown Mental Home in Devon. That such a man should have ended up in a Mental Home being diagnosed with psychosis was bad enough—that he should have died there less than a month after his arrival was even more unbelievable. Yet there was nothing I could do, other than read the brief telegram with sadness, stow it neatly folded in my wallet, and resolve to look into the matter at such a future date as circumstances permitted.

At the time of his demise I was stationed overseas, attached to the embassy of one of our allies, and so it was not until after the cessation of

71

hostilities that I was able to return to England in the autumn of 1945 and make enquiries into the manner of Harvey's passing. What I learned…well, let me merely say that for a man who is not easily shaken, I found myself extremely unsettled.

With little difficulty I was able to locate Dr. Reginald Staines, who had been the medical officer in charge of the home at the time. Dr. Staines had since retired, but I was directed to a small ivy-clad cottage nestled in the hills near Corfe, with a fine view of the romantic castle—one which I had pleasant memories of visiting in the pre-war days with an attractive young woman…but that is another story, and one best left on the dusty shelves of memory.

Dr. Staines, who met me at the door of his cottage, was a wiry, white-haired gentleman, officious in manner, but cordial once I introduced myself and reiterated the reason for my visit, which I had expressed earlier in a letter.

"Harvey Gorton was a friend of mine," I said, "and I should dearly like to know what happened to him."

"It was an unusual and disturbing case," he replied, ushering me into a book-lined room obviously used as a study, and instructing his housekeeper to prepare a pot of tea. "I remember it well."

"Disturbing?" I queried.

Dr. Staines planted himself in a leather-backed chair across a sturdy walnut desk, and motioned me to an upholstered armchair closer to the warmth of a crackling fire.

"In two ways," he said, stroking his chin and looking serious as only a medical professional can. "In the nature of his delusion, and in the manner of his death."

"What was his delusion?" I asked, thinking to begin first with the malady.

"He believed," Dr. Staines replied, folding his hands, "that he was being hunted by a woman, a Princess Bessenyei."

I laughed. "We should all be so lucky as to be pursued by a princess."

His smile was mirthless. "On the contrary, he was very afraid of this princess. Terrified, in fact. He could hardly bear to utter her name."

"Harvey was always the most level-headed of men," I said, perplexed. "I never heard of him having a fear of women."

Dr. Staines nodded. "In all other respects he was completely normal. We had many enjoyable talks together. He was very well-informed, and very fond of Hungary and its people. He hoped—in vain, as you know—that Hungary would escape the late war."

The housekeeper arrived with a tray bearing a pot of tea and biscuits which she deposited on the desk. She poured two cups, dropped a cube of sugar into Dr. Staines', and then departed.

"What of the manner of his death?" I asked, adding cream to my tea before sipping it.

Dr. Staines pursed his lips. "He had fallen on a snowy day and broken his humerus. During the examination by the surgeon, the chain of a small crucifix that he wore broke, and he became so agitated that he needed to be sedated. The crucifix was initially forgotten, but later found when the room was cleaned, and locked in the Matron's desk. Sometime in the evening, while I was visiting with the vicar, a foreign woman appeared and asked to visit Mr. Gorton. She was placed in a waiting room while my deputy was consulted, but upon the nurse's return, she had vanished. Shortly thereafter, a terrible scream came from Mr. Gorton's room. The staff rushed in, and found him dead."

"How?" I asked quietly.

"It was most curious. The body had been completely drained of blood."

I set my cup down with a rattle. "Had he been stabbed, or his throat cut?"

Dr. Staines shook his head. "Nothing of the sort. The only wound I could find was a small double puncture on his neck—hardly worth noticing. And there was not a drop of blood on the bed or the floor. It was most curious," he said again.

I felt a sudden unease. "What was your hypothesis?"

He appeared embarrassed. "I really couldn't formulate a good one. My best guess was that of a sudden haemolytic anemia. Perhaps some kind of exotic poison had been administered..." He picked up a plate. "Biscuit?"

I took a shortbread, although I wasn't hungry. "Is there anything else you can tell me?"

"Not much," he replied. "We were unable to locate any next of kin. The local priest, Father Robertson, performed a Mass and oversaw the interment in St. Thomas' churchyard."

"What of the Princess Bessenyei?" I queried.

"No one ever saw the foreign woman again, if that was she. But since she had given no name, who can tell?"

"Thank you," I said, rising. "You have been most helpful."

Dr. Staines rose as well. "You are quite welcome. But wait -! There is one more thing." He pulled open a drawer of his desk and rummaged inside, eventually extracting a handful of papers. "He wrote this not long before he died, at my request. I don't know that reading about his delusion will be of great benefit to you—I don't even know why I kept this—but if you wish, you may have it. I don't think he would mind, since you were a friend of his."

I placed the handwritten papers carefully in my briefcase, and thanked him again for his courtesy.

"See the castle while you're here," Dr. Staines said before closing the door. "It's well worth a visit."

Normally, I would have followed his advice, but today I was not in the mood to visit ruined castles, no matter how romantic.

I read the papers while the train steamed back to London. It took me some while as the papers were handwritten, and Harvey's penmanship had never been the best.

It was not until the train was pulling into the station that I became aware of being the focus of stares from the other passengers in the compartment—and I realized that I must be showing on my face the horror that I felt in my heart.

I endured a restless night's sleep in which a shadowy, cloaked figure seemed to stalk me through a bizarre landscape of ruined castles and jagged hills under a blood-red moon—a dream which I hoped was only a fantasy born of Harvey's weird tale and not a portent.

I spent the morning pursuing investigations of a confidential nature, then after lunch called upon Father Achilles Rush, a priest of about my own age whom I had known since we were boys. We both had contemplated joining the priesthood; Achilles had pursued that calling, while I had discovered that my vocation lay elsewhere.

Knowing him as I did, I trusted Achilles' judgment implicitly.

Achilles was short and round, the innate cheerfulness of his face concealing an incisive mind. He was also, I knew, a man of deep spirituality as well as being well-read in certain branches of esoteric lore.

He greeted me effusively, as it had been years since our paths had crossed—before the War, as he reminded me. I was surprised to see him walking stiffly with the help of a cane, and he explained that one leg had been severely injured during a bombing attack on London—he'd been crushed by falling bricks while attending to the needs of some wounded.

I expressed my condolences, which he brushed aside with a characteristically good-natured wave of his hand—"I'm alive and have no complaints"—and we spent a good hour—and a liberal portion of excellent brandy—in catching up with each other, before I raised the purpose of my visit.

I briefly explained my connection to Harvey Gorton, relayed Dr. Staines' account of his death, then handed him Harvey's statement, with my marginal clarifications of some of the more difficult passages.

He perused it carefully, offering an occasional "ah" or "hmmm" or some other comment, like "foolish man" or "incredible."

I allowed my eyes to wander around Achilles' small sitting room as he read, thinking what a world away it was from the one revealed in Harvey's papers. Theological treatises nestled comfortably next to the novels of Father Benson and dark, leather-bound volumes with forbidding Latin titles. A depiction of St. Michael the Archangel hung comfortably alongside a portrait of His Majesty King George VI and a faded photograph of Achilles' parents. Various knick-knacks had presumably been tokens of appreciation from parishioners.

Eventually Achilles laid down the pages, removed his glasses and wiped his forehead with a handkerchief, before replacing his glasses and studying me with his deceptively mild brown eyes.

"What do you think?" he asked.

"What do *you* think?" I countered.

"Have you checked into other sources?" he queried.

I nodded. "Harvey was indeed assigned to Budapest before the war to investigate a woman alleged to have been involved in international espionage. But that is all I could determine. The records relating to his mission, his reports, and any documents pertaining to Princess Bessenyei— assuming that any existed to begin with—seem to have disappeared."

"Is that unusual?"

I shrugged. "When dealing with sensitive diplomatic matters it is not unheard of. But in this case I think it curious. Now tell me…"

"If what he wrote is true," Achilles replied slowly and deliberately, "– and that is for you to determine—then I am of the opinion that your late friend became involved with a creature of utmost darkness."

It was not what I wanted to hear. "You believe his story to be true, then?"

"I cannot be completely sure, mind you," he replied, "as I didn't know your friend, but from the way he wrote, my considered opinion is that he was as sane as you or I."

"The doctors thought him to be delusional."

"That wouldn't surprise me."

"But Achilles…" I exclaimed, "dash it all, man, this is the twentieth century, not some dark era of superstition! We are reasonable, enlightened men!"

He looked at me quizzically. "Perhaps we are not as reasonable and enlightened as we like to think we are."

I leaned back in my chair, not sure whether to be relieved that Achilles had supported my reluctant suspicion, or disappointed that his belief now placed a burden upon me.

"Assuming you are right," I said, "—and I still can hardly bring myself to believe it—what do you advise?"

"For you?" he asked, scratching the side of his nose, and I nodded. "I recommend that you destroy these papers and go about your life as if you had never read them."

It was not the answer I expected. I sat upright. "But…but…"

"Are you wondering if something should be done?" he asked, his head tipped to one side like that of a curious dog.

I motioned assent.

"This evil has been haunting the earth for over four hundred years," Achilles said, gesturing with his hands. "Do you fancy yourself the man to defeat it?"

"I thought…with you…the two of us…"

Achilles gave a short laugh. "Much though I value our friendship, it is impossible. The bomb did more damage to me than just mangle my leg. I'm afraid that travel is out of the question. I rarely even leave the confines of my parish."

I felt a momentary fading of my hopes. But then determination rose up again. "Harvey was my friend," I said. "If what he wrote is true, I owe it to him to avenge his death. And not only that, but to prevent further unfortunates from becoming its victims."

"You risk becoming one yourself," Achilles pointed out.

I swallowed. The possibility had crossed my mind. "It's a risk I'm willing to take."

"Then far be it from me to attempt to dissuade you." Achilles rose and limped across the room to an antique cherrywood cabinet which he opened with a small key. "It's likely to be a grisly business," he added.

I swallowed. "I'm aware of that."

"Take these," he said, handing me a small crucifix on a silver chain and a bottle of holy water. "The crucifix was blessed by His Holiness himself. I received it from his own hands when I was in Rome. I pray that it will shield you from dangers the likes of which you can hardly imagine."

"Thank you," I replied, slipping the crucifix over my head.

"On no account remove it," Achilles admonished, raising a cautionary finger.

I shivered inwardly, recalling Harvey's horrible fate. "I won't," I replied grimly.

"The holy water is from St. Peter's." Achilles laid his hand on my head. "May God go with you, my friend."

"I pray so, Father."

"You will be going as a sheep among wolves. As Our Lord admonished, be as innocent as a dove, and as wise as a serpent."

I took a deep breath. "I understand."

Achilles' gaze was both serious and encouraging. "Give me news of your safe return."

"I will," I promised, adding softly, "should I do so."

My next task was to consult with my superiors in London and convince them to assign me to Budapest. This proved to be easier than anticipated, as one of our representatives there had become incapacitated by a sudden illness, and an experienced replacement was required—one, moreover who was not averse to going to a country left in shambles by the war and in which Soviet influence was ascendant. Being tolerably proficient in both Hungarian and Russian only confirmed my suitability.

The Budapest which I entered some weeks later, however—by which time winter had arrived, casting a dreary blanket of gray skies and scattered snow over the entire countryside—was no longer the "noble and romantic city" which Harvey had encountered, with "twinkling lights along the Danube, the great flood-lit statue of St. Gellert, and the eternal gypsy music throbbing through the city."

Instead, I found myself in a ravaged city of roofless buildings and shattered walls where not so long ago people had been eating dead horsemeat found in the streets in order to survive. Not one bridge across the Danube remained intact—the Germans had blown them up to slow the Soviet advance. And as for gypsies—some 28,000 had perished at the hands of the Nazis.

There were signs that life was recovering, even though the political situation remained unstable as various parties jockeyed for power under the watchful eye of Soviet officials reporting to Stalin. I had to walk carefully, and yet my duties were not so onerous that they prevented me from making enquiries about the Princess Bessenyei.

Royal titles were not, of course, much in evidence in the new regime, and for a while my efforts proved fruitless. I was able to ascertain only that a family named Bessenyei had once existed, and that there was, indeed a Castle Bessenyei on the Transylvanian border. But one day in early March, as spring was approaching, at one of those otherwise dreary functions of which the communists were proving themselves masters, I overheard a conversation in which the name of Gizela Bessenyei was mentioned.

I moved closer to the two gentlemen.

"I hear that she is quite beautiful," said the younger.

"I would keep my distance if I were you," replied his companion. "There were stories told of her before the war."

"What sort of stories?"

The man looked around, his glance passing over me as I was examining a hideous modern painting on the wall, and lowered his voice. "Young men who made her acquaintance had the unfortunate habit of turning up dead some while later."

"Dead? But what a way to go!"

"Take my word and avoid her like the plague."

The younger man sighed. "I can dream, can't I?"

"Dream all you like, but if you have an ounce of brains, keep your distance. For the life of me I don't know why Zoltan Tildy invited her next week."

"Did he really—?"

I turned away from the awful artwork and left the room.

Zoltan Tildy was a prominent politician associated with the Independent Smallholder's Party. Utilizing various department contacts I was able to pull some strings and secure an invitation to Tildy's rally.

Although I am not by nature a nervous man, my heart was pounding and my palms were sweaty when a stolid, gray-suited functionary ushered me into the hotel ballroom where the reception was being held. I assumed there would be the usual round of tedious speeches, but a long table laden with drinks promised a modicum of relief. I circulated among the dignitaries, offering such words about the position of Britain on various issues as were prudent, when the conversation in the room behind me suddenly hushed, and I turned to look.

A woman entered the room on the arm of a tall, handsome man.

"Janos Szabo," said the politician to whom I was talking. "Fancies himself as something of an authority on economics."

"The woman?" I asked.

"Gizela Bessenyei. Comes from an old landed family, I understand. Let me introduce you."

I allowed him to lead me closer to the couple, as conversation resumed.

"Janos, may I present you to Arthur Chambers," said my guide. "An English diplomat."

"Pleased to make your acquaintance," said Szabo in heavily accented English, giving me a firm handshake. I replied in the same language.

"Herceqnö"—'Princess'—I said, taking the woman's hand, and thinking how accurate Harvey's description of her had been. A slim woman of medium height, with auburn hair and piercing green eyes, yet with a curious pallor of her face and hands that contrasted with the blood-redness of her lips. She appeared to be about thirty years old, but somehow—and I cannot explain it, for her face bore not the slightest wrinkle—gave off an aura of great age.

"Princess no more," she replied in Hungarian, giving a small smile that revealed oddly sharp teeth. "Simply Gizela."

Her hand was cold, and I let go of it quickly as I bowed.

"The Bessenyeis are an ancient family," I said. "I understood the line to be extinct."

She laughed, but it was like icicles falling to the ground. "I am not extinct, am I, Janos?"

"Certainly not," said Szabo, giving me a dark look from under heavy brows. "Come. We mustn't keep our host waiting."

"We shall meet again," she said to me, and though her words were pleasant I didn't like the calculating expression that I thought I perceived in her eyes. Harvey had been right to be wary of her, I thought, and yet he had succumbed to her influence.

The evening passed in dreary fashion, and I was glad when it ended.

Gizela Bessenyei departed as she had arrived, on the arm of Janos Szabo, and I made my way back to my rooms at the British diplomatic mission.

And, for the next three weeks or so, I learned nothing new except that Gizela Bessenyei was often seen in the company of Janos Szabo. Where she had been before meeting him, I was unable to determine.

Then, I happened to be attending a reception in support of Ferenc Nagy, another politician, when Gizela Bessenyei arrived, this time unaccompanied.

"Where is Janos Szabo?" I asked the party leader. "Isn't he coming tonight?"

"Haven't you heard?" he replied. "Szabo died last week."

I started. "What happened?"

"Apparently he went for a walk in the woods. A woodcutter stumbled across the body. From what I was told, he'd been torn to pieces—by a wolf, or a pack of wild dogs. Nobody seems to know for sure."

I shivered. Not that I'd known the man, but it was a bad way to go.

I sat across the room from Gizela Bessenyei, hoping that she wouldn't notice me, as I felt a strange reluctance to have anything more to do with her—a reluctance bordering on revulsion.

But if I didn't want to approach her, she had no such qualms, catching me before I could extract myself from the loquacious clutches of a rambling old professor and make my escape.

"Mr. Chambers, a pleasure to meet you again," she said.

I forced myself to smile politely. "Princess."

"Gizela, please."

"I heard about your loss."

"We were acquaintances, no more," she said, giving a slight lift of her shoulders.

The unemotional way in which she spoke chilled me.

"Would you see me back to my hotel?" she asked.

There was nothing I would have liked less, but the manners of a lifetime die hard, and I found myself saying "of course," while instantly wishing I could retract the words.

"Excellent," she purred, laying her hand on my arm, and together we passed into the night.

I was on edge the whole way—which wasn't far—expecting any moment for something to happen. But our talk was inconsequential—she asked me several questions about England and what I thought of the new Hungary. Once or twice I contemplated bringing up Harvey Gorton, but something stayed me. After all, what real proof did I have that she was implicated in Harvey's death? He had been visited by a foreign woman, that was all. What evidence was there that this woman had been Gizela Bessenyei? Harvey had undoubtedly met many foreign women in his years in the Service, and I knew next to nothing of his private life.

I bid her goodnight at the entrance to her hotel, and returned to my own lodgings none the wiser. So far, Harvey's tale seemed to be coherent, yet I wasn't fully convinced.

I did what I should have done earlier, and attempted to verify other elements of Harvey's story. His manuscript related that he had enlisted the aid of a certain Professor Otto Nemetz, supposedly a renowned psychic investigator, who had also met an unpleasant death. But there were no extant records of such a professor, and no one seemed to have heard of him. The professor was said to have owned a painting of the Princess Bessenyei claimed to have been painted by one Nicholas Erdösi—who had died in 1502!

Unfortunately, no clues were to be found, and I could only assume that had such a painting existed, it had been destroyed in the war, as had all evidence of Professor Nemetz' existence. Was that likely, I wondered? Could every last scrap of evidence have vanished?

I began to doubt Harvey's veracity.

Surely, I tried to convince myself, Harvey had only seen a painting of one of the Princess' ancestors, and discerned a family resemblance out of which he had spun a web of fantasies. As for her appearance—her pallor and her pointed teeth—perhaps she was suffering from anemia and some dental abnormality—ectodermal dysplasia, I learned from an encyclopedia.

Yes, that must be it.

And yet the nagging fear wouldn't go away. I was a man of two minds, trying to deny what, underneath it all, I somehow knew to be the awful truth.

I encountered Gizela several times over the next few weeks. To my surprise, I felt my initial revulsion waning, despite what I surmised her to be. I am not a psychologist, but I do know that sometimes evil can exercise a peculiar fascination—as if one is mesmerized by a venomous snake, knowing all the time that it *is* a snake—and deadly—but feeling an attraction all the same. Perhaps it is the same as those who willingly court danger. I was, an inner voice warned me, at risk of following in Harvey's footsteps.

Gizela was unfailingly courteous, unfailingly polite, but once or twice I caught an expression in the depths of her green eyes—a look of lusting hunger quickly concealed—that reminded me that I was treading on perilous ground.

"You English are so different from the Hungarians," she said once.

"Have you known any others?" I asked nonchalantly, keeping my tone and expression as innocent as I could.

"One," she replied, regarding me closely. "Years ago…sometime around the beginning of the war." She sighed. "He was a pleasant man, but he returned to England, and I never saw him again."

Was she lying, or was she telling the truth?

"The war caused many disappointments," I said.

"I hope that you won't disappoint me," she said softly, and I felt the force of her seductive powers as I mumbled some sort of response.

I was all but convinced that Harvey had been correct, but—and this despite Father Achilles' pronouncement—still I hesitated. What if, after all, Harvey had been wrong? What if he really had developed a psychosis? His story was *so* outrageous—could it really date back to the fifteenth century and the evil doings of a certain Prince Lóránd and his daughter Gizela who had been executed for murder and Satanism in 1506? Or had he simply concocted an incredibly detailed tale?

I had to be absolutely certain.

What if I impaled this woman on the point of a dagger and was mistaken?

The situation could not continue. And so, in order to obtain full assurance, I decided to journey to Castle Bessenyei to see if what Harvey had written was true, and so put to death any doubts. If I found what he had described, then my way was clear.

I was not so foolish as to travel alone. I chose as a companion Alan McKenzie, formerly a Royal Marine Commando, currently providing security for the diplomatic staff; a man who, having fought the worst of the Nazis, found no terror in the thought of spending a free weekend venturing to a ruined castle on the flank of Transylvania.

A powerfully built man a head taller than myself, with red hair, a bristling moustache, and intense blue eyes, McKenzie appeared amused as I stocked the car with cloves of garlic, a dagger with a cross-shaped handle, and a pair of torches.

"I'd sooner have these, Mr. Chambers," he said, indicating the Colt .45 revolver holstered on his hip, and the Lee-Enfield rifle and electric lamp which he laid on the back seat of the car.

In one sense he was right, as we'd be travelling through regions to which civilization and the rule of law had not yet returned. But in another…what good were bullets against a foe that by all rights should not exist—at least not in any normal sense?

"Let's hope we don't have to use any of them," I said, and he grinned.

We set off, following the map I had marked, and going, as had Harvey, through Kecskemét, Szeged, and Makó. But the war had taken its toll on the countryside, and the going was not always easy. Spring rains had turned unpaved portions of road into quagmires, forcing us to detour many times around impassable sections, and once McKenzie had to clear a fallen tree out of the way. We had brought our own provisions with us, which was fortunate, as otherwise, had we needed to stop for food, the drive would have taken us even longer.

As it was, dusk was falling by the time we reached Makó, and I deemed it prudent that we lodge there for the night. I had no desire to visit Castle Bessenyei after dark. Fortunately we chanced upon a small inn with Spartan, clean rooms, decent food, and a landlord who wasn't interested in two English visitors other than for the money we tendered him.

Perhaps it was the spices or the sauerkraut in the *székelygulyás*—I could hardly blame the *rétes* I had for dessert or the glass of redcurrant wine—but my sleep was troubled. The windows were closed against the chill of the night, and the drapes drawn, and yet I dreamed that a pair of glowing red eyes regarded me through the panes. Part of my mind told me this was manifestly impossible as our rooms were on the upper floor, and yet the unblinking stare of those eyes made me shudder.

Even more disturbing, if that were possible, was the insistent rhythmical tapping upon the glass. Maybe it was only a branch—although I heard no breeze—but it seemed to be a finger tapping to summon me to open the window. Against my will I began to rise, when, perhaps unconsciously, my hand strayed to the crucifix around my neck, and the eyes and the tapping vanished.

Wearily, I fell into a deeper sleep.

Morning found us traversing muddy tracks through cornfields ragged with last year's stubble, and vineyards that had seen better days.

"You've certainly chosen an out of the way place, Mr. Chambers," McKenzie commented as the car rattled and swayed through the dismal countryside.

I had told him no more than that I was looking into details surrounding the death of a colleague. To the Communist authorities—who of course kept tabs on my comings and goings—I was merely a barking mad Englishman interested in old castles.

"If I had my druthers, there are many other places I'd rather be," I rejoined. "I'm doing this out of duty, not for pleasure."

The forest, the periphery of which we skirted, had assumed a gloomy, almost sinister mien. I told myself not to be fanciful, and suppressed the urge to turn around and drive back to Budapest. But the urge grew even stronger after we turned onto the narrow track pointed out to us by a suspicious old man collecting firewood.

"Nobody goes to Castle Bessenyei," he'd said, making the sign of the Cross over his chest.

"It's only an old ruin, isn't it?" I'd asked.

"It's not the castle, but what lives there," he'd answered.

"Spiders? Rats?" McKenzie had said jocularly.

The old man had glowered. "Evil incarnate. Don't say you weren't warned." With the shake of a gnarled finger at us he'd limped away.

"Nothing like a crazy old man to liven up the day," McKenzie said as we bumped up the track. "This country is full of weird tales."

I didn't reply, concentrating on keeping the car on the road which writhed serpent-like between the dark trunks. The forest closed around us, the branches showing no sign of spring greenery, and I was forced to turn on the headlights to see our way. Involuntarily, I shivered.

"Gloomy place, eh, Mr. Chambers?" McKenzie said. "I wouldn't want a castle here."

"Not exactly the bonnie, bonnie banks of Loch Lomond," I replied.

We rounded another bend in the road and in front of us—literally, since they had collapsed and were blocking the way—were the remains of a pair of ruined columns, apparently once part of the castle gate. Some kind of a statue, probably at one time heraldic but now so eroded as to be unidentifiable, lay beside them. I brought the car to a stop, gathered my garlic, and wedged the dagger into my belt. McKenzie and I climbed out, just in time to glimpse something large and gray vanish between the crowded trees.

I opened my mouth, but was precluded by the spine-tingling howl of a wolf—too close for my liking—which gradually faded away.

McKenzie cocked his rifle and swung it to a ready position. "Yon beastie had better not show his face."

I took a deep breath. "Let's get this over with."

We climbed over the rubble of the fallen gateway and made our way along the overgrown drive towards the castle which we glimpsed in the distance. The forest was eerily quiet; only our footfalls disturbed the unnatural silence. Once or twice I thought I caught sight in my peripheral vision of a gray shape flitting through the trees as if shadowing our progress.

What had once been parkland was now an overgrown wilderness of stunted trees surrounding a small, sullen lake. The unsteady remains of a disintegrating bridge crossed a foul moat, and it was with great care that we edged across.

Castle Bessenyei was a truly dismal pile, its sole surviving tower leaning drunkenly, surmounted by crumbling battlements silhouetted against the sky like rotting teeth; its roof sagging like the belly of an old man; and rows of vacant windows staring like the eyes of an idiot. The massive door was shut, but the wood was cracked and flaking.

McKenzie turned up his nose. "No one has set foot in there forever."

"Not quite forever," I replied, thinking that Harvey had spent a night within those decaying walls. "And we're not going to set foot in there, either. I'm only interested in the chapel."

Said building was every bit as derelict as Harvey had described. Normally on entering an ancient church—even a ruined one—I perceived a sense of peace or reverence; due, no doubt, to the centuries of worship and prayer which had been offered there. But this little chapel, dating from about a century before the castle, was different. There was nothing special about its architecture or the shards of stained glass remaining in the windows, yet somehow it possessed a malignant aspect; and as we entered the door it was if an evil miasma filled the interior.

Although it was not yet dark I lit my electric lamp and shone it around the dusty, cobwebbed interior littered with chunks of fallen masonry.

"Down here," I said, indicating some stone steps behind the profaned altar—from which I averted my gaze—that led down to the crypt. McKenzie followed me.

At the bottom I pushed open a wooden door emblazoned with a coat of arms.

A pair of lidless lead caskets standing side by side dominated the small chamber. Tiers of crumbling coffins lined the walls, and spilled human bones lay strewn across the floor. McKenzie kicked bones aside with a rattle that jarred my nerves. I thought to rebuke him for his lack of respect for the dead, but held my tongue.

I looked first at the coffin on the left, and could just barely make out the single word—Lóránd—etched onto the side. It contained nothing but a pile of moldy dust and something cross-shaped. I leaned over, reached inside, and extracted a wicked-looking dagger, just such a one as Harvey had described.

The right hand casket also bore a single word—Gizela.

Steeling myself, and raising my lamp with my left hand, with the dagger gripped in my right, I peered into the second casket, and saw –

Nothing. The casket was completely empty.

Something snarled behind us. McKenzie and I whirled in tandem.

A giant grey wolf stood there, hunched low, fangs bared, tail raised, red eyes blazing, muscles tensed to spring.

McKenzie's rifle roared even as I flung the dagger at the creature.

The wolf turned and bounded up the stairs.

"No!" McKenzie exclaimed. "I couldna' hae missed the beast."

It seemed impossible, at such short range.

I shone my lamp on the steps, but the beams of light showed only our footprints in the dust. There were no blood stains.

"I canna believe it," McKenzie wondered.

"Let's go," I said. "I've seen all I need to."

"Fine wi' me." McKenzie led the way up the stairs, his rifle pointing ahead.

We emerged into pallid daylight just in time to see a gray shape slink into the forest. I thought I heard mocking laughter, but perhaps it was only my overstressed nerves.

"Sure you don't want to look around anymore?" McKenzie said, his tone of voice indicating that the question wasn't serious.

I grimaced. "I've had enough of this godforsaken place."

We retraced our steps across the rickety bridge and the wasteland, both of us scanning constantly for wolves. I breathed more easily once we were safely back at the car—and again once the motor started and we were under way.

I was heartily glad as the gloomy forest with its dreadful castle disappeared behind us. I felt disinclined to talk—and as McKenzie was taciturn by nature, we made the drive back to Budapest in silence.

Once safely within the city limits, I thanked McKenzie for his help.

"Nothing to it, Mr. Chambers," he replied, seeming to have recovered his mood. "Anytime!"

There wasn't going to be another time, of that I was certain.

It was the following weekend when I met Gizela again; a note delivered by a messenger requested that I accompany her to a reception at the estate of a wealthy businessman—one of those whose skills in navigating the black market had allowed him to profit out of the war.

"It has been too long, darling," she said as I handed her into my car. Somehow, the fur coat she wore, while it accented the pallor of her face, also managed to give her features a lupine cast.

"Business," I replied shortly, climbing into the driving seat and putting the car into motion.

"And is there not time amidst the business for Gizela?" she said, her voice wheedling, and her emerald eyes unusually tender.

"You have never been far from my thoughts," I said, and her smile oozed satisfaction. My crucifix was around my neck, and for some reason I'd slipped the vial of holy water into my jacket pocket.

The reception went as tolerably as such things do. Gizela never strayed far from my side. During a lull in the proceedings we found ourselves alone near the refreshment table. The other guests had dutifully traipsed into a side room to listen to the business man's wife play a piece on the piano – being tone-deaf, music held no allure for me. Gizela leaned close, her eyes gazing into mine, her lips slightly parted in invitation. There was seduction in those eyes and in those lips that ever so gently drew nearer to mine.

Despite what I knew, there was something strangely compelling in that unspoken invitation, and against all reason—all sanity—I felt myself being drawn towards those lips, lips that sheltered teeth of wicked sharpness. My resistance faltered.

And then it was as if a voice spoke within me, reminding me that Harvey had yielded to that temptation, and in so doing had sealed his fate.

I pushed her roughly backwards. "I know who you are—*what* you are!"

Her eyes moistened with hurt. She took a step towards me. "Why, Arthur—"

I fumbled to extricate my crucifix from beneath my shirt and held it in front of me. She halted. Her eyes frosted into cold emeralds, and her lips curved in a mocking caricature of a smile.

"Are you a Catholic, Arthur?"

"I am."

"I should have guessed." Her smile became positively malicious. "Do you think I'm afraid of a piece of metal?"

"No," I said, "but of what it represents."

Her laugh was a ghastly parody of humor. "You cannot resist me. Take it off and kiss me, and share my existence forever."

"Never!" I stumbled backwards, one hand keeping the crucifix in front of me, the other reaching behind.

"Come," she said, moving closer, the force of those glittering eyes fixed on me, the hunger in them nearly overpowering.

"Never!"

"You cannot hide behind that crucifix forever, Arthur. I have been alive for four hundred years. I am patient. In my own time I will come for you."

"You have no hold over me!" I said desperately.

She sneered. "You're a fool, like all of your kind. You have no conception of my power."

I kept backing away, feeling as though I was in a bizarre dance with this unclean creature, a dance that could only end in the death of one of us—as Father Achilles had warned me. I wished with all my might that he was here now.

I bumped into the table. Something stabbed into my hand, and I jerked around—letting my crucifix drop onto my shirt as I did so—to see that I'd cut myself on the point of a carelessly laid knife.

In a flash, she had gripped my arm, raised my hand to her lips and sucked the blood. Too late, I yanked my hand away.

"Now you are mine," she gloated, "forever. Even as your friend was."

I stared in disbelief and horror at the blood oozing from my hand. I raised my eyes to see it smeared on her red lips. Blood—that symbol of life, now spelling my doom. All I could think of was Harvey...Harvey and the gruesome death he had died...the death that might now be mine...and what awaited after that...

...to be her creature, forever...

I staggered away, through the open French windows onto the patio, and leaned against the balustrade for support, gasping for breath.

Never, in all my life, had I been so close to despair as in that moment. I felt utterly abandoned, forsaken. It was as if the gates of Hell had fallen and crushed me—or opened wide to admit me to a realm of hideous torment.

And she was there, my nemesis, her gown whispering in the breeze; this abomination; this embodiment of treachery and rebellion against God and nature; this denial of everything good in humanity; this undead creature existing as a parasite upon the living.

"It's not so bad, is it, Arthur?" Her voice mocked me.

My mouth was dry. "I need a drink," I said, the trite words all that would come to my mind.

Gizela regarded me with scorn. "Fetch me one too, Arthur," she said.

Numbly, I weaved back through the French doors over to the drinks table. "God," I prayed silently, fingering my crucifix, "what has happened to me? Is there to be no escape? Do not let the powers of evil have the victory. Save me, I beg you."

Gizela, I knew, drank only aerated water, and I reached for an opened bottle. It was as I poured a glass that, in a sudden burst of inspiration I knew what I must do.

Casting a quick glance to make sure that she wasn't watching—she stood with her back to me, looking out over the terrace—I pulled the vial of holy water from my pocket, unscrewed the top, and emptied the contents into the glass of aerated water.

"Judgment day," I murmured *sotto voce*, then put the vial back into my pocket.

My heart was pounding as I brought the glass back to Gizela and handed it to her, hoping she wouldn't notice anything amiss about my demeanor.

"Thank you, darling," she said, raising the glass and draining it.

Suddenly, her eyes widened, the expression mutating from puzzlement to dawning understanding. If I had thought to glimpse a flicker of repentance *in extremis*, or a shred of humanity—perhaps manifesting itself in a plaintive "Arthur, what *have* you done?"—I was to be disappointed. This was an utterly depraved soul that had long been given fully over to evil.

Faster than it takes to describe, the dawning understanding gave way to full realization and then bitter hatred. The glass fell from her hand and shattered on the tiles.

Not only her eyes, but her entire visage burned with malevolent fury.

"God," I said, feeling suddenly strong, "will not be mocked."

Her mouth opened in a scream of pure rage. She lurched for me, her arms extended, her hands clawed in spasm. Mere inches away from me she froze in mid-movement. Her face turned as gray as a weathered tombstone and then developed a multitude of tiny fissures like craquelure in an old oil painting. Even as I watched they widened and spread. The process seemed to go on forever, but could only have been a matter of seconds.

Her mouth yawned wider and her eyes blazed a final defiant glare as I stood paralyzed.

And then she crumbled into a pile of ashes.

I let out the breath I hadn't realized that I was holding.

It was long moments before I became capable of movement, and then I started at the sound of a man's voice.

"You missed a good performance." The businessman was standing behind me. "Where is the princess?"

I forced words through my tight throat. "She was called away unexpectedly," I replied, conscious of a warm wetness on my hand. My wound had begun bleeding again, as if to wash away the foul touch of her lips. "Do you have a plaster?"

"Why, you are injured!" the businessman exclaimed. "Of course, my friend. Come inside."

We re-entered the room. On the patio, a spring breeze blew the ashes into the darkness of the night.

eight

THE MAN WHO COLLECTED GODS

"Any guesses as to why I invited you?" my friend Conrad Roberts asked, handing me a glass of iced lemonade and a straw before tipping his head to one side and raising his bushy Einstein-like eyebrows.

We sprawled in canvas sling chairs on the deck of his Florida beach house looking out over the placid Gulf of Mexico. A squadron of pelicans cruised barely above the wave-tops, while the sun dipped towards the horizon, splashing the clouds with vivid hues of gold and scarlet and lengthening the shadows of a young boy playing ball with his dog at the water's edge.

I took a long swallow of the refreshing drink, thinking that it had been too long since I'd last exchanged the stress of my clinic and the bustle and traffic of Orlando for the relaxation and tranquility offered by the seaside.

"Most likely because you've acquired a new item for your collection," I replied languidly. "That's the usual reason."

"Try harder," Conrad encouraged.

He was wearing a cap emblazoned with a vegvisir. "Iceland?" I guessed.

"Close," Conrad said. "Come inside."

"Must I?" I complained, loath to leave the comfort of my chair and the refreshing sea breeze.

He rose and motioned me to follow.

I sighed, set down my lemonade, and gained my feet. Truth to tell, I preferred the exterior of Conrad's house to the interior. Conrad was a collector. Had he collected model trains, or stamps, or horse figurines, or any number of other things, I wouldn't have minded. But no, he collected gods—effigies, statues, carvings, and reliefs of divinities and sundry other related supernatural beings.

And again, had he confined his interests to Jesus and Mary and the saints, I wouldn't have minded. But his fascination ranged much farther afield than that.

Jesus and Mary and a variety of saints were indeed present, but they rubbed elbows with Horus, Anubis, and Thoth; Odin, Thor, and Fenrir; Marduk, Ishtar, and Tammuz; Jupiter, Juno and Pan; Zeus, Venus, Apollo, Athena; Huitzilopochtli and Quetzalcoatl; Viracocha; Krishna and Shiva…a virtual pantheon of more deities than I could ever remember.

Some of the pieces, I grant, possessed considerable artistic or historical merit. Others simply gave me the shudders, particularly those associated with death. I could barely stand to look at Shezmu clutching his butcher knife dripping with gore; Kali draped by her necklace of human skulls; goat-headed horned gods of fearsome aspect…

Especially when the illumination caught them just right and their inlaid eyes seemed to glow with infernal fire. I wanted nothing more than to cover my vision and flee.

Call me squeamish if you like, but it was a visceral reaction over which I had no conscious control.

"Nothing so terrible today," Conrad grinned, knowing of my aversion to that aspect of his collection and steering me past what I called the 'nightmare room' into the 'saint room.'

Conrad, I might mention, was a stickler for order, and had partitioned his collection between the various rooms of his house. The 'saint room' had been one of the spare bedrooms, overlooking the dunes, now modified with display cases and shelves lining every wall.

Conrad climbed onto a stepstool—he was barely over five feet tall—plucked a figure from a shelf and handed it to me.

It was about eight inches tall and carved out of some sort of dark soapstone. It depicted a bearded man wearing a toga or chiton, with sandals on his feet, and holding either a pen or some other implement in his right hand. It was, in my admittedly inexpert estimation, quite an ordinary representation of a Greek or Roman man of the first centuries AD.

And yet...despite the lack of any unusual characteristics, there was something indefinably disturbing about it. I couldn't say why, but I didn't like it. Holding it gave me a queer feeling in the pit of my stomach.

"Is it ancient?" I asked.

Conrad had been busy cleaning his glasses during my examination of the statuette.

"I don't believe so," he said, replacing his glasses. "Sixteenth or seventeenth century would be my guess."

"Where did you get it?"

"From an antique dealer in Trondheim. It was supposedly found at the site of Sverresborg Castle over a hundred years ago."

"Doesn't it belong in a Norwegian museum, then?" I asked.

He laughed. "Maybe if it had more of a provenance. According to the dealer, a man whom he didn't recognize brought it in one day saying that it had been in his family for generations. The dealer put it for sale without any guarantee as to its authenticity. But when I saw it, I knew it belonged here."

I handed it back to him, reflexively wiping my hands on the sides of my shorts.

"Did you notice the writing?" he asked.

I hadn't.

"Look here," Conrad said, indicating some faint makings on the base. "You can just make them out. There's an 'L', a blank where a letter has been worn away, a 'K' then another blank."

"L-K-" I repeated.

"Luke, don't you think?" Conrad asked. "The good physician."

I shrugged. "Could be, I suppose."

Conrad laughed as he returned it to its place at the end of a shelf next to a sixteenth century carved wooden head of St. John the Evangelist.

"In your honor," he said, "you being a physician of sorts yourself, I shall present several outstanding requests to this fellow."

"My honor doesn't matter," I said, dismissing his gentle needling. "Praying to a statue won't accomplish anything."

He scowled. "I mean the aspect of divinity behind the statue, of course," he replied. "Really, Larry, your constant dismissal of such religious inclinations as I possess can be quite tedious."

"I just think they're overly broad," I said.

"Sorry, Larry," he replied. "Like Pilate, I don't believe that truth can be so tightly pinned down."

His cheeks had flushed. Normally, Conrad enjoyed a good argument, and we'd been friends for so long that neither of us took offense at what the other said. But today...

"Maybe we should talk about your health then," I said as we headed back onto the deck, I being quite glad to exit his house of horrors.

"That's the first thing I shall pray for," Conrad said, sounding calmer. "I've had this tingling in my left leg for months now. It drives me crazy at night, and my doctor hasn't been able to do a thing about it. I shall ask for it to be removed. A physician saint should be able to do that, don't you think?"

"That sounds like a reasonable request, I suppose," I conceded.

"I'm glad you approve," Conrad said, with the merest hint of sarcasm. "How about a walk on the beach?"

"Fine," I agreed. Anything to put some distance between me and the disturbing statuette—my hands still felt funny, as if I'd been handling a snake.

I recalled that conversation some three months later when I happened to be passing the area on the way to a conference in Tallahassee, and decided to pay a call on Conrad. We'd had no communication in the interim, which wasn't unusual.

Conrad seemed thinner than when I'd last met him, his cheeks sagging and grip weaker.

"Is everything all right?" I asked, when we were seated on the deck.

"It's been a rough time," he replied, running a hand back over his straying hair.

"Leg still bothering you?" I continued. "I noticed that you've got a bit of a limp."

"It doesn't tingle anymore," he said.

"That's good then, surely."

"If you consider this to be an improvement." He pulled up the leg of his slacks to reveal the shiny metal of a prosthesis.

"Conrad!" I gasped, nearly falling out of my chair in shock. "What happened?"

He motioned towards the beach. "I was walking barefoot on the sand and stepped on something. Next thing you know, I've got this flesh-eating infection travelling up my leg."

I whistled. "You're lucky to be alive."

He gave a crooked smile. "That's what the surgeon said. It was lose the leg or lose my life. And I wasn't ready to do the latter."

"You should have told me! I might have been able to help."

He waved the suggestion away. "You know me. Too private by half."

"I hope it doesn't keep you down for long," I said.

"I hope not either," he agreed. "I'm heading up to New York in three weeks."

"Why's that?"

"I want to unload a painting I picked up a few years ago," he said. "Foolish me, I found it tucked away in a flea-market in Amsterdam, and thought it might be a genuine old Dutch Master."

"Do I assume that it wasn't?"

He puffed out his cheeks. "Well, the canvas was period, but the signature was a forgery. So it was an anonymous painting of no exceptional merit."

"Then why take it to New York?" I queried.

"Because I might get something for it. And because I want to look at some galleries for other additions to my collection."

I laughed. "I might have known." And then, for some strange reason, I added, "and don't forget that St. Luke is the patron saint of artists, as well."

Conrad pursed his lips. "Maybe I'll give him a second chance. See if he can wangle a few extra dollars from an art dealer."

"Good luck," I said. "Give me a call when you get back."

He nodded absently, then we talked about other things, and after a while I took my leave.

But not, I confess, without a sense of unease, the reason for which I couldn't quite identify.

I decided, rather than simply hear a verbal account of Conrad's trip to New York, to visit him upon his return and take him a gift—his birthday was coming up, and I was concerned about his ability to cope with his disability. Conrad had never been the healthiest of men, and I feared that the trip to New York would take more out of him than was desirable.

So having ascertained the date when he'd be back, I made an arrangement to visit him. However, a series of unforeseen events occurred—my car was rear-ended, the water-heater gave up the ghost, and a colleague unexpectedly quit. Due to these delays, it wasn't until a month after Conrad's return that I was able to head once again to the Gulf coast.

If last time he had seemed physically down, this time it was mental. He had that sallow cast of features and monotonal intonation of a person who is sick at heart.

"Didn't it go well?" I asked, taking my usual seat on the deck.

"I found a couple of nice items," he said, waving his hand limply in the direction of the house.

"But what about the painting?" I wondered. "Did you sell it? Did St. Luke help you get a good price?"

"Oh, I sold it," he replied without spirit. "Not a lot, but worth the trip."

"You don't seem very happy about it."

He indicated for me to stay put, then went into the house and returned with a newspaper which he handed to me. "Did you see this?"

He'd folded the page to reveal one story. *Unknown Vermeer Discovered.* "Yes, I remember reading—"

Understanding dawned. "You don't mean—"

Conrad nodded glumly. "Underneath my anonymous painting was a genuine Vermeer. Worth millions. And I sold it for a few thousand."

No wonder the man looked ill.

"I brought you a present," I said setting the newspaper aside, and removing a small box from my pocket. "It's not much."

He opened the box and extracted a clay Roman lamp. "It has Diana on it," I said, although surely he could tell that at a glance.

"Thank you," he said, sounding more polite than excited. "It's a nice addition to my Roman collection."

I followed him into the house, pausing to look in the 'saint' room while he took the lamp to the Greco-Roman room. I was surprised to see the statue of St. Luke lying on the floor. I looked up at the shelf, and…

Had the head of St. John moved over?

It certainly wasn't quite where it had been before.

"Conrad!" I called. "Did you know your statuette is lying on the floor?"

He came up behind me as I bent to pick it up.

"I must have knocked it off when I was dusting," he said. "Careless of me. Good thing the floor's carpeted."

"It appears undamaged," I said, turning it over in my hands. As I did so, I had the same strange, disturbing sensation as when Conrad had first showed it to me. But why?

I was used to seeing statues of the Holy Family and various saints in church. So why did this statuette purportedly of St. Luke bother me?

"Put it back up, would you?" Conrad asked.

I moved St. John over a few inches and replaced St. Luke in his proper position. "Could it be older than you think?"

He shrugged. "I suppose so, although I doubt that it's older than Medieval. Why?"

"Just wondering. I think you should get rid of it."

His jaw dropped. "Whatever for?"

I struggled for words. "There's something wrong about it…I don't like it."

He laughed. "There's a lot of my collection you don't like."

"True, but—"

"Besides, as a physician you should appreciate St. Luke."

"It's not that I don't appreciate him, it's just that…I can't explain it, Conrad. It doesn't feel right to me."

He was shaking his head and I could tell that I wasn't getting anywhere.

"You've been inhaling too much anesthesia," he said. "Besides, there's one more thing," he continued. "Other than physicians and artists, who is St. Luke the patron saint of?"

I racked my brain. "Ah…goldsmiths and butchers, I think. And maybe brewers…notaries comes to mind…something else?"

"Bachelors," Conrad said decisively. He touched his chest. "I've been feeling lonely. I need some love in my life."

I exhaled, knowing people who'd had bad experiences on internet dating sites. "Just don't get taken for a ride."

"No fear, Larry."

Well, Conrad was a mature man, able to take care of himself, and so there was no reason for me to be unduly concerned about his romantic prospects. His love life was no business of mine. And yet I was worried. Perhaps my feelings arose simply out of long friendship—we'd known each other since college, when we'd been soccer teammates. And though our lives had taken very different paths—he making a fortune in real estate, me pursuing a career as a plastic surgeon—we'd always remained in touch.

I telephoned him a couple of times, but he was always noncommittal in his replies. Was this a good sign or a bad one? I didn't know.

Eventually curiosity got the better of me, and since the remote approach hadn't worked, I decided that a personal visit was in order—if nothing else I could scope out signs of a love affair…a letter, flowers, new clothes…anything out of the ordinary.

And so under the pretense of coming for a day's swimming—true enough, as swimming had always been one of my passions, and the Gulf provided a change from my pool—I took myself to Conrad's house.

He was as affable as ever, although it soon became very obvious that he was well aware of the true reason for my visit. He kept me waiting until after I'd been swimming before indulging my curiosity, however.

He handed me a Bahama Mama once I'd changed back into street clothes, and followed it with a small slip of paper.

Love will soon be knocking at your door.

It was followed by a list of numbers and a Chinese symbol.

"Is this from a fortune cookie?" I exclaimed. "Please tell me that you're not putting any credence in that?"

"It's not enough that you disparage my little saint," he smiled, "now you disbelieve my fortune cookie as well?"

I relaxed. "You had me going for a minute, there."

"But it's an interesting coincidence, don't you think?" he said, retrieving the paper.

"I bet there are millions of cookies with that message," I replied, taking a long pull at my drink.

"We'll see," he said. "We'll see."

We made small talk and finished our drinks, and I was getting ready to leave, when the doorbell rang, followed by a loud knock.

"I didn't know you were expecting company," I said.

"I'm not," he replied, preceding me to the front door. He opened it, to reveal a pair of rather bulky men in dark suits and shades. One of them flashed a badge.

"Jason Love, FBI," he said.

"You have got to be kidding!" Conrad exclaimed.

The leading man removed his shades and stared at Conrad, his expression cold. "Are you Conrad Roberts?"

"Yes," Conrad said.

"We want to ask you a few questions."

"What is this about?" Conrad asked, moving aside to allow the men to enter.

"We're attempting to trace some artifacts looted from the National Museum of Iraq that may have come to America," Love said, looking around.

"All my items were acquired from reputable sources," Conrad protested. "I have receipts and documentation—"

"That doesn't mean the dealers acquired them legitimately," Love said. "We want to examine your collection and your paperwork."

I cleared my throat. "I think I'll be leaving you gentlemen," I said.

"And who are you?" Love asked, turning a searching gaze at me.

"An old friend," Conrad interjected, "who is totally ignorant of antiquities."

I pulled out my wallet, extracted a business card, and handed it to Love. He scrutinized it, then put it in his breast pocket. "We'll be in touch," he said.

"Later, Conrad," I said, taking my leave, little knowing there would be no later.

Conrad sent me a card informing me that the FBI hadn't found anything indisputably suspect in his collection but that they were 'continuing to investigate.' That, I would have assumed, should have been somewhat reassuring to him. So the call from the Law Office of Meyer & Meyer, which came to me while I was at work one day, took me completely by surprise.

"Conrad dead?" I exclaimed. "He didn't…it wasn't suicide, was it?"

The lawyer explained.

When Conrad's mail began to pile up, the postal carrier had contacted the police. They'd broken in to find Conrad dead on the floor. The coroner's verdict was that he had caught his prosthetic leg on an edge of the carpet and fallen, striking his head against a large bronze Buddha. He'd apparently never regained consciousness.

Did I want to hear the relevant portion of his will?

"Certainly," I replied, sitting down at my desk to absorb the shock.

Conrad, having no close relatives, had appointed me executor. As recompense for this task, I was to receive such contents of the 'saint' room as I desired. The remainder of his collection, except any items of disputed legal status, was to be donated to museums or sold.

I had a hard time concentrating for the rest of the day, to the detriment of my patient relations and the consternation of my staff.

As soon as I was able, I went up to Conrad's house to begin the process of disbursing his possessions, thankful that he'd catalogued his extensive collection. The dwelling seemed curiously empty, but also creepy, as those ancient gods and goddesses stared at me with their sightless eyes.

I hurried to the 'saint' room.

And no…it couldn't be.

St. John had moved over again, and the statuette of St. Luke was lying on the floor.

I picked it up—and with an exclamation nearly dropped it again.

Then, shuddering, and with my heart pounding, I carried it out behind the house and smashed it to pieces with a hammer.

St. John gazes benignly on me as I sit in my study writing this. He gives me comfort—while also reminding me of poor Conrad. But despite his reassuring presence, I can never erase the memory of what I saw when I picked up that awful statuette.

For no longer was it the image of a grave, first-century man clad in a toga or chiton. It had changed, and the figure wore a belted tunic, cloak, and tall, fur-trimmed boots. The face was still bearded, but narrow, with a pointed chin and a horrible, leering expression that made me feel ill.

And on the base…

The vowels between the 'L' and 'K' had become visible—and they weren't the 'U' and 'E' which would have formed the name of a saint.

Instead, I had clearly made out an 'O' and an 'I'.

LOKI.

nine

THE WELL

Wells have always fascinated me. As a child I was attracted to those dark, stone-lined shafts which, like tunnels, fostered in my youthful mind visions of unknown, mysterious places. Whenever my parents took me to visit a castle, I would always head straight to the well and peer through the protective grating down into the dank, watery depths.

What secrets did they hold? What lay beneath the inky surface of the water?

Was there lost treasure? Weapons with magical powers? Human bones? Ancient amulets? Dire inscriptions?

The dungeons, which fascinated my brother, or the views from the summits of the pigeon-infested towers which my sister loved, held no interest for me. Neither did the gift shops favoured by my friends, with their wooden shields and swords, toy soldiers, and colouring books.

For years I tried and failed to find a rational reason for my attraction. Eventually, though, an explanation presented itself. But to this day I'm still not sure I believe it.

Because to do so would mean either to doubt my sanity or to accept the validity of an ancient curse.

I met Lucinda Hadley when she entered my uncle's bookshop in the village of Upper Wyton one bright day in April. Uncle Alfred, while vastly knowledgeable in the antiquarian book trade, was absolutely hopeless when it came to finances. An urgent plea from my Aunt Ethel had brought me over from Hereford with the aim of bringing order to his accounts before the minions of Her Majesty's Revenue and Customs latched onto his deficiencies.

Being a lover of books myself, although in a more casual way—turn of the century novels in the tradition of Guy Boothby, and Victorian ghost stories—I was minding the store while Uncle Alfred went out to buy cigarettes; indulging a habit against which Aunt Ethel had railed futilely for years.

I was perusing the pages of Adam de Cardonnel's *Picturesque Antiquities of Scotland,* first edition, 1788—which, since it bore a price tag of £750 I handled very carefully—when the bell hanging on the inside of the door jangled.

I hastily replaced the book into its locked display case behind the desk and turned to greet the customer—and caught my breath.

She was nearly as tall as I, and about my own age of thirty-five, with chestnut hair cascading to her mid-back, fine-boned features, and a slender figure worthy of a model. She wore a green Irish shawl over a patterned blouse, a knee-length skirt and leather calf-boots.

"May I help you find something?" I asked, mesmerized by her eyes, a light-grey like morning mist.

She seemed nonplussed. "Isn't Mr. Stanfill here?"

"He stepped out for a few minutes," I replied. "I'm watching the store for him. I'm his nephew, Philip Stanfill."

"All right then," she said briskly. "He has a book reserved for me. Under Lucinda Hadley."

"The title?" I asked, moving to the shelf of reserved books.

"*History of Tewkesbury*," she said, "by James Bennet."

I ran my finger along the spines, then pulled out a thick volume. "Here it is. 1830." I removed a file card sticking out. "£100."

She took it from me and flipped through the pages.

"You're interested in local history?" I asked.

"Very much so," she replied.

"Is your family from this area?"

"They've lived in Hadley Hall for over four hundred years," she said, glancing up.

"Not too many people seem to be interested in history anymore," I commented. "The younger generation doesn't care. They're too preoccupied with the latest computer games and   gadgets."

"So true," she said, closing the book and handing it back to me. Her nails were neatly manicured. "It's nice, but don't you think £100 is a little steep? There's quite a bit of foxing on the pages, and the cover is water-stained."

"I suppose my uncle has his reasons for the price," I said, since although I loved to read I knew next-to-nothing about pricing antique books.

She looked disappointed, and the overwhelming urge to please this woman came over me.

"What do you think would be reasonable?" I asked.

She put a finger to her bronze-tinted lips. "65?"

"Done," I said, thinking that I'd make it up to Uncle Alfred.

"I've never seen you here before," she said, "and I've been a customer for years."

"I live in Hereford," I replied, handing her the receipt to sign and putting the book into a bag. "I just come over every now and then. Right now I'm helping Uncle Alf with his accounts."

She handed the receipt back and our fingertips touched. Something like an electrical shock went through me, and I could tell by the sudden wideness of her eyes that she felt something as well.

"Thank you," she said, pivoting quickly for the door.

"Is there anything else you'd be interested in?" I asked.

She paused momentarily and adjusted her shawl. "I'll call if anything comes to mind."

Then she opened the door and was gone.

I leaned against the counter, feeling suddenly weak.

"You all right, Phil?" A man's voice accompanied the banging open of the door.

"Fine, Uncle," I said, as a short, stocky man in a black-and-white rugby shirt and jeans came over to the desk.

"I saw Cinda Hadley crossing the street."

"She picked up her book."

"Nice girl," Uncle Alf said, subsiding into his creaky old chair. "Good customer, too."

"And very pretty," I added.

His eyes twinkled. "Have an eye for the ladies, do you?"

"Anything wrong with that?"

"Nothing at all," he chuckled. "She normally comes in on a Friday. About two."

I smiled back. "Thanks for the tip."

I returned to Hereford with a sense of anticipation not entirely due to the improving state of Uncle Alf's financial records.

As the head of my own accounting firm, I enjoyed the luxury of being able to adjust my schedule as desired; in this case so as to return to Upper Wyton—only an hour's drive away—the following Friday.

But to my disappointment, Lucinda didn't come.

In fact, it wasn't until three weeks later that she reentered the shop. It was a dreary Friday, with a chill rain sluicing down from heavy clouds, gushing through drainpipes and pouring off slate roofs, and running in streams along the street, soaking the feet of the few shoppers who hurried along under sagging umbrellas. I almost hadn't come, thinking it unlikely

110

that anyone would be buying books in such inclement weather. And indeed, customers had been few and far between—and tourists, at that.

Uncle Alf watched reruns of Jeremy Brett as Sherlock Holmes on the small telly he kept on the front desk, while I worked on accounts in the back room.

The doorbell tinkled, and I heard Uncle Alf say, "Miss Hadley! Did you take a boat to get here?"

A musical laugh answered him. "No, but I might need one to return home again."

I closed the account books and stood up.

"I have something you might be interested in," Uncle Alf said. "Just arrived yesterday. Where did I put it?"

Rummaging noises emanated from the desk area. I picked up a book from a stack of new arrivals, and carried it into the front shop where Lucinda Hadley stood, looking like a Venus newly emerged from the sea, although clad in a dripping leather raincoat.

"Is it this one?" I asked, handing the book to Uncle Alf and giving Lucinda a smile which she returned with a hint of surprise, and, unless I imagined it, a welcoming light in her grey eyes.

"*Collection of Gloucestershire Antiquities* by Samuel Lyons," Uncle Alf said, glancing at the title page before passing it on to Lucinda. "1804. It's not in very good shape, I'm afraid, so I can let you have it very inexpensively…"

She gave it a cursory examination. "It will do for a reading copy."

"Beastly weather, isn't it?" I said, as Uncle Alf took the book to wrap. "Just the day for a cuppa at the tea shop around the corner."

There was the flicker of a pause during which my heart skipped a beat or two before she replied, "That would be brilliant."

"Wonderful!" I hurried to put on my jacket and cap.

"Take your time," Uncle Alf said as we headed out.

Tea and Dorset apple cake in the cozy environs of Aunt May's Tea Shop proved conductive to conversation, which ranged from details of my occupation to a common interest in music—I being a halfway decent amateur pianist while she played the clarinet—to books we had both read and enjoyed, to places we would like to visit. Both parties were sufficiently pleased with the outcome as to arrange a dinner date for the following week.

After escorting Cinda to her silver Vauxhall Astra VXR and watching her drive away down the puddle-filled street, I returned to the shop to find Uncle Alf reading a book.

"Get on well?" he asked.

"Magnificently," I said.

"Good," he replied. "I can't believe I never thought to introduce you before. The Hadleys of Hadley Hall were an influential family in the district at one time. Wealthy, too."

"Not now?"

"Shouldn't think so. It's a big old place to keep up."

"With priest holes and ghosts?"

"Hidden rooms, probably. Ghosts?" He shrugged. "There are stories about most of these historic homes. I expect if you researched far enough back you'd uncover some mystery to do with Hadley Hall."

And on that note, as the weather was worsening, I bid goodbye to Uncle Alf and motored back to Hereford, paying less attention to the road than I ought to have, as my mind was filled with thoughts of Cinda Hadley.

That dinner proved to be the prelude to subsequent exploration of local culinary establishments. Over the subsequent weeks Cinda and I discovered that we shared a variety of interests, from investigating archaeological sites to hiking on the hills (rain or shine) to browsing the back rooms of dusty antique stores to enjoying afternoon tea and cream cakes at outdoor cafés.

One day, I invited her to Hereford; I showed her my office and introduced her to the staff, and then we visited the chained library in the Cathedral. Most of the books are, of course, theological in nature, but Cinda, who was acquainted with the curator, was permitted to allow me to examine an ancient volume of local history.

"This is the oldest reference to Hadley Hall," she said, indicating a small yellowed drawing surrounded by columns of print.

Due to the expense of maintaining a property as old and extensive as Hadley Hall, Cinda had informed me that her parents had transformed one wing into a bed and breakfast. Cinda, with a degree in business, handled the management.

"Has it changed much?" I asked.

She shook her head. "Very little, really. A few trees have been removed, while several more have been added. My family has always been very careful to preserve the original appearance of the house and grounds as much as possible."

I laughed. "It makes the Stanfills sound like the newcomers we are. The closest to a family estate we had was a row house in Liverpool."

"Truly?"

"Truly. My grandmother must have hated it—she was from this area somewhere, but ended up in Liverpool when she married my grandfather."

"You haven't mentioned much about your family," Cinda said as, holding hands, we exited the cool dimness of the Cathedral into the glory of a sunny afternoon.

"It's not a happy story," I said. "My grandparents are all gone. Two from cancer, one from pneumonia, and one from a heart attack. They died when I was young, and I never really knew them. My parents were killed in an automobile accident while I was away at university. My brother lost his life in a military training exercise, and my sister moved to Italy. I haven't heard from her in years. My mother was an only child, so that leaves Uncle Alfred as my sole near relation."

She gave my hand a squeeze. "I'm so sorry. I have aunts and uncles and cousins galore. I can't imagine what it must be like to have so little family."

"One manages. Adjusts."

"You're very pragmatic."

"Realistic," I countered. "Speaking of which, how about dinner before you head back to Upper Wyton? The Red Lion has an excellent carvery."

"It sounds delightful," she said. "But it's high time you met my parents. Next week, you must come to Hadley Hall."

"I can hardly wait," I accepted eagerly, having no intimation of the strange occurrence that lay in store for me there.

Cinda was waiting in the arched, ivy-covered entryway as I drove up the curved gravel drive past a large oak tree and parked beside a splashing fountain in front of Hadley Hall. Neither the picture I had seen nor her description did it justice.

Built of grey stone with a slate roof, the Hall exuded an air of permanence, as if proclaiming that though people would come and go, the building would remain. Asymmetrical wings flanked the entrance; one of two stories, the other of three. Neatly tended flower beds and bushes broke up the severity of straight lines and served to nestle the building into a landscape of green lawn and weeping willows.

Cinda greeted me with a kiss. "Welcome to my home, darling."

"It's lovely."

"Would you like to see the grounds before we go inside?" she invited.

I motioned. "Certainly! Lead the way."

We strolled through a rose garden, skirted the right-hand wing, and then circled behind it, finally reaching the rear of the Hall. We halted beside a glass conservatory.

"This is a Victorian addition to the original building," Cinda said, "most of which dates from 1590, although a couple of rooms were added in the seventeenth century."

A wisteria-wrapped pergola sheltered a table and chairs, and overlooked a sequence of terraces that tumbled down a hillside like a series of waves, ending beside a small, rush-bordered stream.

"It's idyllic," I said, before catching sight of a circular stone structure about three feet high on the far side of the uppermost terrace. Heedless of Cinda's "Wait!" I hurried across and peered into it. I couldn't see the bottom, just the courses of mossy bricks descending into blackness.

"It's the original well," Cinda said catching up to me. "There's still water in it, although it hasn't been used for close to a century. When I was a little girl it was my wishing well. I don't know how many pennies might be down there. Until one day my nanny caught me, gave me a spanking, and told me—"

I'd only been half-listening, when suddenly a tide of dizziness surged over me. It felt as if the well was slowly circling…and with it came a sensation—a very strange, disturbing sensation…

I lurched forwards—

"Philip!" Cinda exclaimed, gripping my shoulders. "Are you all right?"

I pushed myself back from the well and turned to face her. "Just a little dizzy…"

Cinda was regarding me with a worried expression.

"Let's get you inside," she said, taking me by the elbow and steering me towards a rear entrance.

As we approached the house, the dizziness faded almost as quickly as it had come, and by the time she ushered me into a comfortable sitting room, it had gone completely, although the sensation of something not quite right persisted. She settled me into an easy chair.

"I'm fine now," I said. "Don't know what came over me."

I was half-tempted to return to the well to see if the reaction occurred again, but my better judgment decided against such an imprudent action.

"Dinner will be ready shortly," Cinda said, "Let me find my parents."

George and Violet Hadley were a charming couple of about seventy, and we enjoyed lively conversation over a rack of lamb, roast potatoes, and carrots. Whatever had bothered me at the well hadn't affected my appetite.

"We've heard a lot about you," George Hadley said.

"All of it good, I hope," I replied, to which Cinda said, "Except for supporting the wrong football club."

"For which allowance can be made," George chuckled. "I've told Cinda for years that she needed someone in her life besides her mother and me. I'm glad that you seem to be fitting the bill." He raised his wine glass. "Here's to more evenings together."

My eyes met Cinda's. "To many more," we said in unison.

115

I pondered the incident at the well—and the strange feeling it had engendered—as my car purred homewards along the dark roads. Upon reflection, it seemed to me that the sensation I had encountered was as though the well had wanted me and had sought to draw me into its dank, fetid depths.

It was most peculiar.

No, not peculiar. It was frightening.

I shivered, and turned the heat in the car up a notch.

But surely, I told myself, dizziness wasn't unusual—maybe I hadn't eaten or drunk enough at lunch. And as for the weird attraction, perhaps it was the effect of bad air on a mind already fascinated by wells.

Even as I pondered this, the same disquieting urge that I had felt at Hadley Hall rose up within me—the compulsion to turn around, despite the lateness of the night, and return to the well. It was as though I were a character in a horror film, being drawn unwillingly towards something unknown and unimaginable.

My rational mind did its best to squelch such inclinations. I told myself that Hadley Hall was a normal house inhabited by normal people. Something had disturbed my imagination, that was all.

The odd feelings subsided when I pulled into the drive and entered the familiar surroundings of my house. I read a chapter of a novel and had a small drink to help me relax.

But my rational mind could do nothing at night when the unconscious assumed control.

I dreamed that I was leaning over the well, reaching for the coins that Cinda had dropped into it as a child, coins that glittered and shone far below as if in inviting me to gather them.

I stretched my arm as much as it would go, leaned farther and farther, but always the coins were just out of range. And yet I knew I had to reach them…they were there, so far and yet so close…if only my arm was just a little bit longer.…

But then I was falling, plummeting headlong into the well, the shining coins coming closer and closer—

And then I hit the water—

—and woke up, to see the reflection of city lights on the ceiling above me.

I gasped and slowly regained a sense of reality.

But even as the dream dissolved, I had the fading sensation that the well had been calling to me, not audibly, but inwardly, and not benignly, but for some dread purpose that I couldn't discern.

I had never dreamed like that of a well before.

And I hoped I wouldn't again.

It was perhaps a month before I returned to Hadley Hall. A business matter took me to Exeter for a week, then the illness of a junior partner compelled me to assume his work…and so it went. Cinda came up to Hereford a couple of times, and we conversed daily, but I was thrilled when I was again able to drive down to Upper Wyton one Sunday.

I parked my car in the shade of the ancient oak that spread its branches towards the Hall and hurried to join Cinda in the conservatory.

After a light lunch we went for a ride along the lanes on a pair of her father's horses, then sat under the pergola for lemonade and biscuits.

It was a thoroughly pleasant afternoon, although I couldn't help but regard the well with a curious mixture of attraction and distrust. If Cinda noticed me viewing it warily, she said nothing.

We retired to the music room when clouds rolled in, Cinda insisting that I employ my modest skills on the piano until it was time for dinner. By then, though, a full-fledged storm had developed, and we ate to the accompaniment of the wind whistling around the eaves like a bevy of disinterred ghosts.

"I should go before it gets too much worse," I said after polishing off a helping of sticky toffee pudding, and eyeing the lashing branches through the dining room windows.

"It's a frightful evening to be on the road," Cinda said, reaching up to lay a hand on my shoulder as I set down my spoon and climbed to my feet.

"Yes, but there's work in the morning," I replied as George fetched my jacket. "I don't like to inconvenience clients."

"Why not drive up early?"

"But if a road is blocked…" I said. "A downed powerline…" She looked disappointed, but agreed. It was as we were saying goodnight in the entrance hall that a loud crack sounded from outside. I opened the door to see that a large branch had fallen from the oak tree.

Not only was it lying across the drive, effectively blocking it, but it had landed squarely across the roof of my 1980 Triumph Spitfire convertible.

"Well, I guess that settles it," I said, shutting the door against the wind.

"How dreadful!" Cinda exclaimed.

"It's a car," I replied.

"Now you'll have to stay the night," she said. "There are several unoccupied rooms in the guest wing—you can have one of those."

"Breakfast included?" I asked, grinning.

"Full, of course," she smiled back.

And so we stayed up late chatting and listening to music while the wind howled and rain intermittently spattered against the windows.

The en-suite guest room—"Aunt Maud's Room" according to a brass plaque screwed onto the door—was furnished in a manner designed to appeal to the desire of American tourists for an "olde world" experience. Still, it was charming enough and the bed very comfortable. I had no doubt that I would sleep well, especially once the gale had blown itself out.

And so I did, for a while.

But sometime in the night I dreamed again of the well.

I was out on the patio, with the moon shining from between strands of cloud, and the merest hint of dawn lightening the eastern horizon. The flagstones, littered with fallen leaves, were cool under my feet, and the stones of the well's edge damp under the palms of my hands.

The shaft was merely a pillar of blackness extending into the earth. No light glimmered in its depths, and not a sound emanated from its recesses.

It was silly to be afraid of an inanimate object, and yet fear clutched at me, wrapping icy tentacles around my heart and paralyzing my will. I knew that it wanted me, and that its desire could not be denied.

With that strange sense of motion common to dreams, I hitched my right leg over the rim and leaned forwards, ready to fall into the darkness that called to me—that yearned to clasp me in its watery embrace—

At last I would learn the secret of my lifelong fascination—

I spread my arms as if to float downwards—

When a scream pierced the night and an unseen force pulled me backwards—

"No!" my dream-voice protested. "Let me go! It wants me…I must go…"

But the force was too strong. The well receded until it vanished, and with a sense of frustration my dream faded away…

I awoke with a start, a feeling of disorientation, and a pounding in my head. Daylight streaming through lace curtains made my eyes water and I blinked to clear them. It took a moment for me to realize that I wasn't in bed, but on a couch, with a cushion beneath my head and a blanket covering me. I swung my legs to the side and sat up, instantly regretting the movement.

"Are you all right, darling?"

I looked up to find Cinda standing over me. She appeared tired and drawn.

"Other than a nuclear explosion inside my skull."

"Let me get you something," she said, moving away.

I rubbed my temples. It finally dawned on me that I was in the living room of Hadley Hall.

Cinda returned with a glass of water and a couple of pills which I swallowed.

"What happened, Cinda?" I asked. "Why am I here and with a most awful headache?"

She sat beside me and took my left hand in both of her own. "What do you remember?"

I pressed my free hand to my forehead. "I was sleeping soundly, then I dreamed about the well—I think I was going to jump into it—and then something pulled me back. That's all I recall."

She made an indeterminate sound.

"And then I woke up here. Was I sleepwalking? I've never done that before."

I noticed that the hands holding mine were trembling.

"What were the surnames of your parents?" she asked.

The question took me by surprise, but I answered, "My father, obviously, was a Stanfill. My mother was a Russell."

"And those of your grandparents?"

"Cinda, what is this all about?"

"Tell me, Philip!"

I took a deep breath. "My grandfather Edward Stanfill married Betty Edgar." I watched for her response, but she motioned for me to continue.

"My maternal grandfather James Russell married Miranda Hastings—"

I caught her as she turned pale and swayed. "Cinda!"

"No," she moaned, "It can't be! It can't be!"

"What's the matter?" I asked, turning her chin towards me and staring into her anguished grey eyes. "What is it?"

"I have killed you!" she cried, burying her head against my chest. "Philip, I've killed you."

It took a few moments for me to recover my poise.

"Cinda, I'm very much alive," I protested, holding tightly to her shuddering form.

She studied my face. "You don't know, do you? You have no idea!"

"No idea about what?"

"The Hastings curse."

"I've never heard of it."

She got up, crossed over to the bay window, and stood with her back to me. I went to stand beside her. The window looked out over the terraces…and the well.

The well.

Something quivered inside me at the sight of it, and I averted my gaze.

Cinda cleared her throat.

"I'll tell you the story," she began. "The history of the Hadleys and the Hastings goes back centuries. They were neighbors, and their fortunes and misfortunes frequently ran in parallel. Occasionally there were conflicts and misunderstandings, but for the most part the relationship was one of friendship and frequent intermarriage."

"So we might be distantly related?" I queried. "That's not a problem."

She waved away my interruption. "That's not the point. It was in the last decade of the 1700s that serious trouble arose. A son of the Hastings was enamored with a daughter of the Hadleys named Annabelle. Normally, no one would have objected to such a marriage, but Louis Hastings was a rake and a wastrel—a dissolute youth who spent his time hunting and playing cards and squandering his inheritance on loose women and drink. Despite this, Annabelle Hadley was infatuated with him—Louis was apparently quite handsome and dashing—and, well, to put it bluntly, he got her pregnant.

"The proper course of action at that time would have been for him to marry her. But Louis pointedly refused. Annabelle told her parents, and they pressed the young man, but he denied that the child was his. There was a fearsome row. Louis' parents took his side—"

"Not very fair," I said.

Cinda said, "Historical records are scant, so a lot is conjecture. But it may be that they were concerned for the girl's welfare—not wanting to see Annabelle marry a good-for-nothing like their son. I have the impression that they were planning to pack Louis off to Australia.

"Whatever the truth, it became an ugly affair. Emotions were running high on both sides, and Annabelle was facing disgrace. And then one day she disappeared."

"Scarpered?" I guessed.

"If only. They finally found her at the bottom of the well, thanks to one of the family dogs that would sit there and howl."

"That well?" I asked, once again looking out the window.

Cinda nodded. "It was never determined whether she flung herself in during a fit of despair, or whether Louis threw her in to get rid of her, since she was last seen arguing with him in the gardens one evening.

"Regardless, the Hadleys were devastated—and furious. So furious that the girl's grandmother, who was supposed to have strange powers—she was reputed to have Celtic blood and was born within sight of a stone circle—pronounced a curse on the Hastings. It went like this:

'If Hastings come, consider well

The shameful death of Annabelle;

'Til knot is tied and flowers fall,

Hastings shall drown at Hadley Hall.'"

I sniffed. "Not exactly great poetry."

"Wait until you hear the full story," Cinda said. "Louis himself was the first victim. The gamekeeper spotted an intruder lurking around at night and took a shot at him. In his haste to escape, the intruder blundered against the rim of the well—it wasn't as high then as it is now—and toppled into it. When they fished the body out, they discovered it was Louis. Why he was there at night was anyone's guess."

"Poetic justice," I said.

"And then Squire Hastings himself succumbed. He'd come to Hadley Hall to dispute the encroachment of some farmhands onto his property and got into an argument with Mr. Hadley and his foreman. The dispute escalated, both men being somewhat short-tempered, pushing and shoving ensued, and Squire Hastings tumbled backwards into the well."

"An accident," I commented.

"No charges were brought, but needless to say, relations between the Hadleys and the Hastings cooled considerably. Each family kept to themselves. But a generation later, when memory of the curse and the unfortunate events which led up to it had faded, another Hastings fell in love with a Hadley. He rode his horse up the terraces to pay court, but the animal shied at something and pitched him into the well."

"Again, an unfortunate mishap," I said.

"People were now talking openly of the curse," Cinda said, twisting her fingers together. "And when it happened a fourth time—to a Hastings cousin who paid a clandestine visit one night and was only located because a fragment of his cloak was found dangling on the edge of the well, even the scoffers were silenced."

"All very interesting," I said, "but this happened a long time ago."

"True," she agreed. "But time wasn't good to the Hastings. High Hollow Court, their ancestral home, burned to the ground in 1849. The family, what was left of them, scattered. A Hastings hasn't come to Hadley Hall in a century and a half."

She covered her face with her hands. "If I'd known you had Hastings blood, I'd never have brought you here!"

I took a deep breath. "They might all have been accidents," I said, trying to sound reassuring. "And really, just because I had a bad dream—"

"You didn't," she said softly.

"Of course I did!" I exclaimed, despite a sudden doubt that crept into my mind.

"I woke up early," Cinda said, "nothing unusual, as sometimes I go jogging then, and happened to come out through the conservatory. I saw you perched on the edge of the well and screamed. Fortunately Ned, the gardener, was nearby and grabbed you just as you began to fall in."

She shuddered. "It was the curse, Philip, and I have brought it on you."

I could hardly bear the bleakness in her eyes. I put my arm around her shoulders.

"Cinda, we're modern people. We don't believe in ancient curses," I said with more confidence than I felt. "But I will keep far away from the well, I promise you."

She wiped a tear from her cheek. "It won't matter. No one has escaped the curse."

I thought about the strange perception I had had. The odd dream. The unconscious attraction to the well that had brought me there at night.

The weird pull that, despite my revulsion, still tugged at me.

"You must never come here again," Cinda sobbed. "Perhaps if you left England…went far away…"

"Would you come with me?" I asked.

"In a heartbeat. But would the curse accompany me?"

Would it? Would the attraction—the compulsion—follow me? Would it stalk me wherever I went, biding its time until circumstance or fate engineered my death?

Could I ever be sure of escape?

Or would worry gnaw at me forever?

The words of the curse had burned themselves into my mind, and I repeated them silently:

If Hastings come, consider well
The shameful death of Annabelle;
'Til knot is tied and flowers fall,
Hastings shall drown at Hadley Hall.

Then I spoke the last two lines out loud, as a flicker of hope blossomed.

I clasped Cinda's hands and pulled her close. "Do you love me?"

"Of course I do, Philip."

"And I love you. Marry me, Cinda! Right now."

"Philip," she said, pushing me back to arms' length, "this is hardly the time to be joking—"

"I'm perfectly serious. 'Til knot is tied and flowers fall. Tying a knot obviously refers to marriage—"

"And flowers fall?"

"When the bride throws the bouquet. Cinda, we can make reparation for the evil committed by my ancestor, heal the breach between the

Hadleys and the Hastings, and end the curse!"

Her long hair swung as she shook her head. "But...but we can't arrange a priest or a church that quickly—"

"So we'll have a civil wedding now and a proper church wedding later."

She pursed her lips. "Hadley House is an authorized venue. And the registrar knows us well..."

Her eyes brightened. "It might work."

"And I promise you a proper proposal and ring."

She laughed. "Let me make some phone calls."

"Cinda," I said, casting a nervous glance out the window as she turned towards the door. "Don't leave me alone."

Occasionally, even the most petrified bureaucracies can be persuaded to work quickly. The registrar was most accommodating, and a wedding was performed in the presence of Cinda's astonished parents, the equally astonished Uncle Alfred and Aunt Ethel, and the house-staff.

When it was over, George Hadley gave me a firm handshake while Violet congratulated her daughter.

"Glad to have you in the family, Philip," he said. "Even on short notice. I'll never understand why the younger generations are always in such a rush."

I'm sure I had a foolish grin on my face. "Sometimes fortune must be seized quickly," I said. "To have gained a wonderful wife and break a curse on the same day doesn't happen to everyone."

"Eh? What curse would that be, then?"

I released my grip. "The curse uttered by Annabelle's grandmother."

He frowned and scratched his head.

"Hastings drowning in the well if they came to Hadley Hall..." I prompted.

He rolled his eyes. "Oh, she didn't tell you about *that*, did she?"

I nodded. "She did."

"Lot of nonsense."

"But—"

"Come over here." He drew me aside to a corner of the room and lowered his voice. "When the children were young, they had a nanny. Odd girl, but a good disciplinarian. She had a vivid imagination and enjoyed telling the children all sorts of fanciful tales. One of them had to do with the well and people drowning in it. Maybe she intended to scare the children to keep them away from danger…"

I could hardly believe what I was hearing. "You mean the story's not true?"

He raised his eyebrows. "I suppose there might be a kernel of truth in it somewhere," he said vaguely. "A lot can happen in four hundred years."

"Cinda lied to me?" I gasped.

"That's not what I—no," he said hurriedly. "She'd never do that—there's not a dishonest bone in her body. The thing is, she's always believed the story to be true. She has an entire library of old books of local history that she pores over, searching for references to the Hadleys and Hastings."

"Then it *could* be true?"

He clapped me on the back. "I wouldn't lose any sleep over it."

I was too stunned to reply.

"You look like you could use a stiffener," George said, heading for the drinks table.

"But—" I began, my mind whirling in a confused tangle of thoughts, recollections of bizarre compulsions, and images of weird dreams—one of which apparently hadn't been a dream at all. Above all the memory, which I would never forget, of the frightened expression on Cinda's face when she thought she'd condemned me to death.

And yet, George…

I shook my head to try to clear it.

I parted the curtain and glanced out the window at the well, now hardly more than a darker patch in the shadow of the house.

Then I looked across the room and saw the radiant smile on Cinda's face. I straightened my collar and went to join her.

ten

THE TABLET OF DESTINIES

It was a somber group that gathered in a reading room of the University library one afternoon some ten or fifteen years ago, despite the beauty of the late autumn day which beckoned through the windowpanes with an unseasonably sunny invitation.

Prescott was a wreck. The black of his suit accentuated the pallor of his haggard features. The lines in his face were etched deeper than they had been a few months ago, and his hair was somewhat greyer, although on that last point my recollection might have been hazy.

But Prescott had changed, and no wonder—a good friend had died in circumstances that were far from clear to the rest of us; a friend whose achievements we had just memorialized in a solemn service presided over by the chancellor.

For a few moments, no one spoke. Then Henshaw asked, "Are you up to telling us about it, Prescott? The papers reported very little."

Prescott stared into his glass of whisky and soda, and his hand trembled. He shifted in his chair. At last he raised dark-circled eyes.

"You were all his acquaintances," he answered with a sigh, "and have a right to know. But what I can offer you probably contains more questions than answers."

"Tell us anyway," Millslow urged. "Whatever you know is better than nothing."

"You might change your mind on that score," Prescott said grimly. "But very well."

He drew a deep, rasping breath and began.

Robin Layman had invited me to join him on a dig at Qadisiyah, on the Tigris in Iraq, near the confluence of the Adheim River. This, I learned, is one of the sites suggested as the location of the ancient Sumerian city of Akkad, which, of course, later became the capital of the Akkadian Empire. I was rather surprised when he asked me to accompany him, as my specialty, Roman studies, does not include ancient Mesopotamian civilizations, and I doubted that I could be of any real assistance to him.

When I expressed my reservations, he laughed and said, "I'll have plenty of helpers, Daniel. I just thought you might like a holiday in the field. See something different. Get away from those Johnny-come-lately Romans."

Well, my own researches had never taken me to the Fertile Crescent, and the idea appealed to me. "In that case, Robin," I replied, "I'd be delighted. Will there be anywhere to play golf?"

"One big sand trap is all you'll find," he grinned. Then he grew serious. "I'm glad you'll come. I'd like to have a witness…just in case."

"In case of what?" I asked.

"Can't tell you," he said, putting a finger to his lips. "At least, not yet."

That was Robin for you. Liked his little secrets.

Had I known what I would be a witness to, I would have thought twice about going. But hindsight, as they say, is 20-20, and I am not prone to premonitions.

I have to admit that the remainder of the semester dragged on—the students were especially dull and uninterested—and then some other matters delayed me, and so it was much later than anticipated when I was finally able to get away. I flew to Baghdad and took a bus to Samarra. It was there that Robin met me, pulling up to the front of my hotel in a dusty Land Rover.

After greeting me, he threw my bags in the back, and pulled out into the crowded city with its streets of squat, square buildings punctuated by occasional wilted trees.

"Do you know anything about Akkad?" he asked, once we had left the city well behind and were bumping along rutted roads past a series of dreary-looking villages.

"Nimrod was a mighty hunter in the eyes of the Lord," I quoted. "His kingdom originated in Babylon, Uruk, and Akkad, all of them in the land of Shinar."

"You know your Genesis," Robin complimented.

"And that's about all," I answered.

"Let me fill you in, then," Robin said, adroitly maneuvering past a stray goat. "Despite being inhabited for two millennia or longer, Akkad virtually vanished from history about twenty-five hundred years ago. Until the discovery and translation of cuneiform tablets, that reference in Genesis was the only clue to its existence. Now, although we have many mentions of it, we only have hints as to its location."

"Which you think is Qadisiyah."

"Yes."

"You sound optimistic."

"I am," Robin said. "And I think I'm on the verge of uncovering something very important."

"Which is…" I prompted.

He held a hand to the side of his mouth. "The Tablet of Destinies," he whispered, although there was no one to overhear us.

"It sounds intriguing," I replied. "And mysterious. When do I get to see this artifact?"

"I can't promise, but in the morning, I hope," Robin said. "It's late, I expect that you're tired, and we'll get you settled in first."

'Getting settled in', once we arrived at the campsite near the dig involved putting my suitcase in a tent and straightening the sheets on a camp-bed. My tent was close to Robin's, with those of the labourers—locals hired to dig—being some distance away.

The dig site itself was an undistinguished mound near the banks of the Tigris, hardly different from any other mound scattered around the plains, and surrounded by smaller hills and irregularities in the terrain. It hadn't rained in weeks, and the scrubby bushes barely made a dent in the sense of desolation that the landscape engendered. Perhaps it was just me, but deserts just aren't my cup of tea, despite a sort of bleak beauty that descends with nightfall.

Robin, however, was in his element. Indeed, he positively exuded an air of restrained excitement. And as you know, Robin was not an excitable man.

"Tell me about the Tablet?" I requested, as we ate bacon and beans beside a flickering campfire. Some of the workmen had returned to their village for the night; the remainder had retired to their own camp, from which we could hear the faint sounds of conversation and singing.

He thought, then nodded. "Like many ancient myths, the story takes various forms, although the broad outlines are the same. I will just tell you one, without wading into the confusing mass of Sumerian and Akkadian deities. The Tablet of Destinies was believed to contain details of fate and the future. It was a clay tablet inscribed with cuneiform writing, and impressed with seals, giving it the status of a permanent legal document. It conferred on its owner—the god Enlil, the Lord of the Storm—his supreme authority as ruler of the world.

"The Tablet was stolen by Anzû—a divine storm-bird that personified the southern wind and thunderclouds—and hidden on a mountain. Sometimes Anzû was pictured as a giant bird that could breathe fire and water, sometimes as a lion-headed eagle, sometimes as half man and half bird."

He got up, went into his tent, and emerged a few moments later with a book, which he handed me. "Here are several renditions of Anzû from various reliefs and friezes."

"I wouldn't want to meet him on a dark night," I said, turning the pages and studying the images.

"Monster, divinity, demon…" Robin said, "whatever he was, the gods feared him. Eventually Anzû was pursued by Ninurta, a god of hunting and war, who slew him with arrows, and returned the Tablet of Destinies to Enlil."

"I've never been in favor of bird hunting," I said lightly, because for some reason I felt uneasy.

Robin gave me a baleful look. "As you might know, hundreds of thousands of cuneiform tablets have been unearthed, but only a fraction of them have been translated. Many are business and legal documents, agricultural records and the like, which frankly are of no interest to me.

"But I was working on a tablet unearthed at Nippur—fragmentary, I'm afraid—which mentioned the Tablet of Destinies and gave me a clue."

"What sort of clue?" I wondered.

"Nippur," Robin said, "was one of the most ancient Sumerian cities, and was the seat of worship of Enlil. The shrine of Enlil went through many periods of disrepair and restoration over the centuries. Nippur has been recently excavated, but no sign of the Tablet of Destinies has been found."

"But it's a myth, surely!" I protested. "You can't really believe that it exists. And even if it did, how would you recognize it among the thousands of other tablets that have been discovered?"

"I have reason to believe it does exist," Robin said, waving aside my objection, "moreover, that it is here in Akkad."

I closed the book and laid it down. "Why?" I asked.

"The last major restoration of the temple was under Ashurbanipal in the mid-600s BC. After the fall of Nineveh in 612 BC, the Temple of Enlil fell into decay. The inscription I read suggested that the Tablet of Destinies was taken into the care of Inanna, otherwise known as Ishtar, who also had a temple in Nippur."

"So why aren't you excavating her temple there?" I wondered, hoping that Robin wasn't going to ply me with a mass of esoteric detail.

"Because Ishtar was the main goddess of Akkad," he said. "And by then, Akkad was likely in ruins, half-forgotten, and a perfect place to conceal the Tablet of Destinies. The inscription hinted as much. I believe that a priest of Ishtar took the Tablet away for safekeeping."

"Robin, it sounds awfully speculative to me—" I began, but he cut me off.

"In the morning, Daniel," he said. "We shall see."

I am not, as I said, given to premonitions, but I have to admit to some ill-defined fears when I left Robin and went to bed. Yet despite them—as well as the heat and the sand flies—I slept fairly well that night, and rose to find that Robin was already up and drinking coffee.

His servant had laid out breakfast for me—Robin having remembered that I was not the man to subsist on mere coffee—and after polishing it off, I followed him to the dig site where his men were already working; but, I thought, with no great enthusiasm.

"What's the matter with them?" I asked, observing the sluggish way in which they removed sand from around a brick wall.

Robin scowled and shook his head. "I can't quite fathom it. They're Muslim Arabs, of course, so their ancestors arrived here millennia after Akkad and its mythology were lost to history. There's not even any folklore associated with the Tablet of which I'm aware. I've heard some of them muttering about djinn, so perhaps they fear that this place is haunted."

"Or maybe someone among them learned of your quest for the Tablet," I offered, "and has been scaring them with tales…perhaps telling them that it's evil and that they'll be cursed by Allah."

He stroked his chin. "I suppose that's possible," he said slowly, "although I've been very circumspect."

"Well, something has frightened them," I said.

"I don't care whether they're frightened or not, as long as the work is done," Robin said, moving to stand by the uncovered mud-brick wall. He gave it a pat. "Here," he continued, "is where I believe the Tablet of Destiny to lie."

I confess that I couldn't see much of interest in the crumbling bricks.

"It looks like any other wall to me," I said.

"But it's not," Robin replied. He drew my attention to an inconspicuous marking. "See this? It's an eight-pointed star, the symbol of Inanna. This was her temple."

I have stood in the ruins of many other pagan temples in my time, gentlemen, and felt nothing, but I confess that this one, despite its innocent appearance, made my skin crawl. Perhaps the workmen felt it as well.

I wanted nothing better than to depart, and leave Robin to deal with his myths and his fancies by himself, but then...curiosity can be equally, if not more powerful, than fear. And aren't we all afflicted with a bad case of professional curiosity?

"There's a very faint inscription as well," Robin said, indicating some other nearly-invisible scratches, "but I can't quite make it out."

"What if it's a curse or a warning?" I wondered.

"Then we're going to brave it," Robin announced.

He motioned to a couple of his workers, and they came and began to chip away at the bricks around the star, carefully removing them one by one.

"Do you hope to become ruler of the world?" I queried. "To control the destinies of men?"

"Too big a job for me, old man," Robin replied cheerfully, stuffing his hands in his pockets. "Fame in academic circles will be quite sufficient."

I'm sure he was being honest, but we're all subject to temptation, right?

The work was slow going, as Robin had to keep chivvying the unwilling men along. I had expected to see nothing but another layer of bricks behind the ones that were removed, but instead—

"There's a cavity!" Robin exclaimed, reaching for a lamp that he had brought.

"Watch out for snakes," I warned, but he shone the light into the darkness.

"It's a small room," he said. "Make the hole bigger," he instructed his workmen, emphasizing his order with sweeping movements of his arms.

When the opening was large enough, he motioned them aside, and wriggled in. I peered past him. At first, all that met my eyes was centuries of dust and sand and rubble.

I could almost sense Robin's disappointment.

And then—"Is that a niche on your right?" I asked, indicating a darker shadow, and Robin said, "By George, I believe it is."

He swept off a layer of dust with a small brush. "There's something here!"

He set down his lamp, reached into the niche, and extracted a large clay tablet. He blew gently on it.

"Let's see what we've got," he said, squeezing back into the daylight with his prize.

I was curious, but the reaction of the workmen caught me by surprise. One of the men who had been enlarging the hole shouted something—I caught only the word *Shaytān*—and threw his pick aside. The other men followed suit, dropping their picks and shovels and fleeing in a babble of unintelligible Arabic. I have to admit that their fright had something of the contagious about it, and I was half-tempted to give in to fear myself.

"Let them go," Robin said, undeterred. "Feast your eyes on this."

To my untrained view it looked like any other clay tablet covered in spikey cuneiform writing. I said as much.

"No," he said, shaking his head. "This is special."

"How can you tell?" I asked.

"This," he said, pointing to a series of robed and crowned figures that marched across the lower third of the tablet, "was made by a cylinder seal. It's probably a depiction of a god—possibly An, the king of the gods and father of Enlil. Maybe Enlil himself."

"And look here," he added, running his finger along a line of symbols. "It's going to take me a while to translate this, but these words—'decreer of fates' and 'lord of destinies'…This is it, Daniel, the Tablet of Destinies!"

He extended it out to me. "Do you want to hold the authority of the gods in your hands?"

I put my arms behind my back. "Robin," I said, not liking the wild gleam in his eyes, "don't you think you should put it back—"

"Are you crazy, man?" he exclaimed. "It's the find of the century!"

"But...but if it really confers the powers you're suggesting..." I motioned feebly.

I could hardly believe those words came out of my mouth—and I can't explain it, there was just a feeling of something being dreadfully wrong...

He glared at me. "If you had just discovered some long lost work— Claudius' histories of Carthage and the Etruscans, say, or vanished writings of Julius Caesar or Suetonius, or how about Agrippina's *Misfortunes*—would you just put it back and forget you'd ever found it?"

"No, but—"

"But what?"

"Those are different, Robin. There's something about this tablet— something unnatural...it doesn't belong here—"

"Nonsense!" he snapped. "Really, Daniel, I expected better of you."

He clutched the Tablet to his chest. "Here is the culmination of my life's work. Scoff if you want to."

With that, he turned on his heel and strode back towards the camp.

I saw no more of him that afternoon. He stayed in his tent, presumably working on translating the Tablet. I wandered morosely around the now deserted dig site. With no labourers left, and with the Tablet of Destinies found, what was there left to do but pack up and return home?

I suppose I should have been glad for Robin, but I wasn't. I couldn't shake an eerie sense of foreboding.

I told myself that I was being fanciful. The Tablet of Destinies was probably some kind of cult object. Perhaps it conferred authority on the chief priest of Enlil. And as for the myth of Anzû and Ninurta...maybe in the distant past some rival for the position of chief priest had stolen it, and a noble warrior had slain the usurper and retrieved the Tablet for the rightful holder. Out of such mundane incidents fantastic legends develop.

My reconstruction made perfect sense, and yet it didn't comfort me.

I prepared supper as best I could while dusk was falling and Robin joined me for the meal. Come nightfall, the sky had clouded over and the wind had picked up. I noticed idly that it was coming from the south. By then, he had recovered some of his good humour.

"How's the translation coming along?" I asked.

"Beautifully," he replied. "It's in archaic cuneiform, which always takes me a little longer."

"So that means it's *very* old."

"Yes. Not long removed from pictographic proto-writing. I can't wait to begin drafting my article on it...you want your name mentioned, old chap? You were there at the discovery."

"Thanks, but that's not necessary," I replied. "I didn't contribute anything."

I noticed that he'd placed a rifle beside his camp-bed.

"Can't trust the locals," he said when I commented upon it. "Once word gets out about a find..."

"They seemed frightened out of their wits."

"I doubt they'll come back. But you never can tell."

He returned to his work, while I went to my tent and read for a while. It was late when I turned down my lamp, but I saw by the glow that Robin still had his burning.

I drifted into a fitful sleep to the sound of sand whispering against the canvas of my tent. I dreamed of old cities and priests and hidden chambers.

But sometime in the night, I was disturbed. The wind had increased considerably and I lay there with the sensation that I'd heard something, without knowing what it was. Perhaps it had been a scream, muted by distance and whipped away by the gale...but it wasn't repeated, and in my drowsy state I thought it might have been a hyena.

And then there was a flapping sound. A tent peg had come loose, I supposed, and a corner of the tent was blowing in the gusts. It was annoying, but I was too tired to get up and investigate and eventually fell back to sleep.

I awoke to a profound stillness. I dressed and stepped out of my tent to find that the wind had died away and the plains shimmered with heat-haze in the brightness of the morning.

"Robin!" I called, before noticing with shock that his tent had collapsed. I chided myself for not getting up in the night. "Robin!" I called again when there was no answer.

I hurried over to the wreckage and lifted up a corner, praying that I wouldn't find Robin lying in the debris.

He wasn't there.

Probably at the dig site, I thought, and jogged over to where we'd found the Tablet. No Robin. I circled the mound, calling his name, but found no sign of him.

The Tablet of Destinies. I hadn't thought to look for it.

I ran back to Robin's tent and searched it thoroughly. The Tablet was gone. But Robin's rifle was still there, as was his notebook.

Had he been abducted in the night? Had some of the workers returned under cover of darkness and made off with him?

Well, there was nothing more I could do there.

The Land Rover was still where he had parked it, and fortunately, the keys were in the ignition. I sped back to Samarra and alerted the police, luckily finding one who spoke passable English.

To cut to the end of my story, they eventually discovered Robin a mile away. He was quite dead, with great gashes across his chest, and multiple broken bones.

He'd apparently been beaten severely, so severely that it was as if he'd been dropped from a great height, according the doctor who performed the autopsy. No trace was found of the Tablet of Destinies. The verdict was death in the course of robbery by person or persons unknown.

Here, Prescott stopped, and took a long drink. Henshaw and I met each other's gaze, neither of us knowing quite what to say.

"Are you suggesting—" Millslow began.

"I'm suggesting nothing," Prescott said, looking from one to the other of us. "I'm not a mythologist. But I wonder if myths ever really die...if perhaps they return, for good or for ill..."

"That's ludicrous!" Millslow exclaimed.

"Maybe so," Prescott said, and his eyes were haunted. "But omitted from the official report was any mention of the tracks that I saw beside Robin's tent. *The tracks like those of a giant bird...*"

eleven

THE POWER OF THE DOG

BLAM!

So close that I nearly dropped the basket of apples I was carrying, the shotgun blast shattered the quiet of the early evening and sent birds squawking from their branches. Before the reverberation had faded, another shot followed.

I set the basket down on the old, moss-covered stone wall that separated my orchard from a swath of Elder Preston's woods and clapped my palms over my ringing ears.

What was the wretched man shooting at? It wasn't hunting season as far as I knew, although not being a hunter myself, I could have been mistaken. Perhaps a rabbit or squirrel had aroused his ire. It wouldn't be the first time.

I shook my fist in the direction the shots had come from, annoyed at the violent destruction of the pleasant, relaxed mood that picking apples had created.

My hands trembled, and I rubbed them together, wincing because I'd managed to abrade several fingertips. I halted the movement at the sound of something crashing through the underbrush.

Elder Preston burst into a clearing, fumbling to reload his shotgun as he ran. His hair was disheveled, his jacket torn, face pale.

"It's after me!" he gasped, turning wild eyes in my direction before looking back over his shoulder into the darkening woods caught in that mysterious time as the sun set and the full moon rose.

"What is?" I called out.

"The dog! *The dog!*" He practically screamed the words as his stumbling steps carried him across the clearing and back into the trees.

I bent over to pick up my basket. As I did so, I had the sensation in my peripheral vision—it was nothing more—as of a shadow rushing past. I looked up quickly, but saw nothing other than a few red and yellow leaves fluttering to join the layer already carpeting the ground.

My skin goose-bumped, and I pulled up the collar of my sweater as the air seemed suddenly cooler.

"You old hypocrite," I murmured as I resumed walking towards my house. "Serves you right."

Another blast from the shotgun came from a distance.

Then a cry.

And then silence.

That was the last time I saw Elder Preston alive.

And I smiled...

"It was built in 1852," the real estate agent informed me, when I first arrived in the area. We climbed out of his car parked in front of an old stone farmhouse located in the hills between Saugerties and Tannersville. "It needs some work," he added apologetically.

I caught the unspoken implication. There were better, more expensive options available.

"I prefer to call it TLC," I replied, and when he gave me a skeptical look, added, "My father was a building contractor. I learned a lot at his side. I'm not afraid of a handyman special."

He made a conciliatory gesture. "No offense, Miss Aalgaard. If you can handle tools, I expect you can handle the neighbor, as well."

"Is he dangerous?"

"Not physically, no."

"Troublemaker? General nuisance?"

"Let's just say that Elder Preston isn't well liked in town."

"I'm not here for the neighbors," I replied. "I'm here for peace and quiet."

"You'll have plenty of that," he replied, as we circled the vacant house, its empty windows gazing forlornly across overgrown fields and orchards. The air was fresh and clean; much better than the city air I'd inhaled for too long in Manhattan.

"Is there a Mrs. Preston?" I asked casually.

"Not any longer," he replied. "Died three or four years ago. Blessing if you ask me."

"Why's that?"

"You'll understand when you meet Preston."

"Give me a heads-up?"

He sighed and studied his clipboard. I could almost see the wheels turning in his head. What would keep the client happy—to speak ill of the neighbor or say nothing? Either might threaten the sale.

"Well?" I prompted.

"Tough as old shoe-leather and about as appealing," he said at last. "Sanctimonious old fraud, if you want my honest opinion. Talks religion all the time, but you'll never catch him lifting a finger to help his fellow man."

"Got it," I said. "Religion's not my thing. But I can throw a Bible verse or two back at him if I need to."

A porch extended across the front of the building. I climbed the steps and turned to soak in the view towards the Hudson River, shining like a silver ribbon winding through a green-velvet valley. A perfect place to put a table and chair, and sit with my laptop and a healthy dose of inspiration. And tea and brownies.

"What is it you do?" the agent asked.

"I'm a writer," I replied. "Ghost stories, mainly."

He unlocked the front door and pushed it open. "Plenty of them in the Hudson Valley."

"Any in this house?"

"None in the listing, anyway," he chuckled, ruffling the papers on his clipboard. "Is that good or bad?"

"Good," I replied. "I just write about ghosts. I don't have any desire to meet one."

My steps on the hardwood floors echoed hollowly in the empty rooms that smelled of dust and old polish. I assessed the possibilities, making a mental checklist as I went. A fresh coat of paint...replace a couple of windowsills...new light fixtures...some area rugs...updated appliances in the kitchen...refinish the mantelpiece over the impressive fireplace...

The stairs creaked as I went upstairs. Bedroom...adequate. Bathroom...needs remodeling. But oh...the perfect writing room, with a bay window and another fireplace for the cold winter days...

"What do you think?" the real estate agent asked when I returned downstairs.

I paused and looked back as we left the house—and a sensation came over me; for a moment I felt as if somehow the house was welcoming me, like an abandoned shelter dog gazing hopefully into the eyes of a prospective master.

"It's just what I'm looking for," I said. "Let's put in an offer."

And so that spring I became the new owner of Adamskill Farm.

I gave no thought to Elder Preston for the first month or two, as I was too busy moving in and making my new house into a home. But one day, when I was satisfied with my progress, curiosity prevailed over aversion and I decided to amble across and introduce myself.

If Elder Preston was severe, so was his abode. Hailey House presented a cold, forbidding face to the world, and as I walked up the long driveway it felt as if an air of oppression hovered over the building and property. As I drew closer, I saw that I was being observed by a dog—a German Shepherd—seated on the small porch beside the front door.

The dog stood and barked, and though it was wagging its tail and didn't seem aggressive, I halted at a prudent distance, and called out, "Hello! Is anyone home?"

In a moment, the door opened, a harsh voice said, "Quiet, dog!" and a man emerged onto the porch.

I wasn't sure what I'd been expecting, but certainly not someone who appeared to have stepped out of the previous century. Elder Preston was thin almost to the point of emaciation, with a narrow face composed of sharp angles and inlaid with a pair of diamond-hard blue eyes. A trimmed goatee perched on his chin, and his long, graying hair was tied with a bow at the base of his neck. He wore a high-collared black shirt and dark pants.

His right hand cradled a shotgun, tipped back over his shoulder.

"Who are you and what do you want?" was his greeting.

I swallowed, wondering if I'd made a bad decision to come over here.

"I'm Nicola Aalgaard, your new neighbor," I replied. "At Adamskill Farm."

He relaxed marginally, and rested the shotgun against the wall of the house. "I heard someone had moved in."

"I just thought I would introduce myself—"

"And see if the stories they tell in town are true?"

"Not at all—" I began, taken aback by his accusation.

He cut me off with a slashing motion of his arm. "Not that it matters. I don't care what people say about me. 'They made their hearts like flint so they could not hear the law.'"

The shepherd whined and he spurned it with his foot. "Enough! Lie down."

"That's a fine looking dog," I said, as the shepherd lay down with its nose on its paws. "Lovely coloring." Rather than the more common tan with a black saddle, the dog was coal black on the back, but tan on its belly. Melanistic, I believe is the term.

"And that's about all," Preston said. "A useless pain, otherwise."

"What's his name?"

"Her. Chika."

"That's unusual."

"She was my late wife's dog. She's gone to her eternal reward, bless her soul. But I suppose you know that."

I nodded. "I'm sorry—"

"Don't be. In due course, I shall join her, as one of God's elect."

"Well," I said, having already had quite enough of this man, "I'd best be going."

"Good day to you," he said. He picked up his shotgun and pushed the dog out of the way of the door.

"Miss Aalgaard—" he called after me.

I stopped and turned to face him.

"Stone walls make for good neighbors," he said.

"Fine," I said coldly, and made my way back down the driveway, conscious of Chika's eyes following me.

Although I generally slept well in my new home—which, as I had hoped, turned out to be the perfect place in which to indulge my literary muse—I woke up that night with the strange sensation of having heard something, but not knowing what. I lay in bed hearing nothing but the normal creaks and groans of the house and the ticking of my mantle clock. After a minute, I threw back the sheets, got up, and opened the window.

The night was still, the trees standing in motionless, serried ranks. From far away came the faint hoot of an owl, but that hadn't been what had disturbed me.

No—there it was again! This time I heard it clearly—the mournful howl of a dog.

A lonely howl...from Chika, I supposed.

It rose and fell on the night wind—and then abruptly stopped. I waited, but it didn't recur, and I went back to bed.

But I didn't sleep; I lay under the warmth of the blankets, studying the patterns in the wooden ceiling-boards.

I met Elder Preston several times over the next couple of months, once or twice in town—where, I observed, people made a point of avoiding him—but more typically when his rounds of his property brought him along the border of mine. Chika would be with him, slinking submissively by his side on a short leash, as if waiting every moment for a harsh rebuke or the blow of a hand.

Never once did I see the dog look happy, although a property such as Preston's should have been a dog's paradise.

"Do you ever let her off to play?" I asked once. "I bet she'd love it."

"The dog doesn't need it."

"Of course she does!"

His mouth twisted unpleasantly. "I might have guessed that you'd be one of that sort."

"What sort?"

"The milk of human kindness sort."

I clenched my hands. "What's wrong with that?"

"'Do not mortals have hard service on earth?'" he intoned. "'Are not their days like those of hard laborers?'"

I felt my temper rising. "Dogs are intelligent beings with feelings and emotions," I said stiffly. "They should be treated with love and compassion—"

"What does the Good Book say? 'For outside are the dogs and the sorcerers and the immoral persons and the murderers and the idolaters, and everyone who loves and practices lying.'"

"It also says 'The righteous man cares for the needs of his animal,'" I retorted.

He wasn't swayed. "She gets food and water and shelter. That's enough."

"Hardly!"

"That's what the law says," he replied, and stalked away, Chika looking back at me with mournful eyes until a sharp jerk on her leash forced her head away.

"We'll see about that," I said to myself.

Unfortunately, that was indeed what the law said, as I discovered when I paid a visit to the Animal Control officer.

"Do you have any physical evidence of abuse?" she yawned after taking down my name and address.

I thought of the harsh words and shouts that I sometimes heard, and the occasional painful yip.

"No," I confessed. "Just verbal."

She shrugged. "I'm sorry. There's nothing I can do."

I wrote Elder Preston into a story and brought him to a gruesome end at Saugerties lighthouse, but it didn't make me feel much better.

One day while prowling around Saugerties in search of inspiration, I chanced upon a bookstore tucked away in an old building on a quiet side-street. I'd made the acquaintance of the local bookstore owners, both in search of material to use as the basis for stories and because I wanted them to stock my books, but I'd overlooked this one—which was a shame, because with its teetering stacks of old volumes, it struck me as being the perfect place to uncover some juicy local legends. Besides, it smelled of antiquity, and old paper, and peppermint.

I was in luck.

The owner, a chatty, middle-aged woman named Laurel, was happy to oblige me.

She poured me a cup of chai tea, swept a clutter of books off an upright chair that had seen much better days, and in answer to my query, said, "There's a legend of a dog...a black dog."

I settled down and sipped the tea. "I love dog stories."

"Back in the late 1700s or early 1800s," she began, "a man named Chosen Preston lived at Hailey House. Are you familiar with it?"

I grimaced. "I live next door."

"Then you know Elder Preston."

"We've met," I said. "The encounters weren't very agreeable."

She nodded sagely. "They never are. If you think Elder Preston isn't the most pleasant person, Chosen, by all accounts was worse. Harsh to both man and beast—unforgiving to his neighbors, not sparing the whip on his horses, and sometimes turning it on his servants.

"In fact, he whipped one of them so badly for a trivial offense that it was feared the man would die. He recovered, but was crippled forever."

"How awful!" I exclaimed, setting my cup down.

"The whole family's like that," Laurel said. "Chosen's sons were no better than their father, and so on down to Elder. Thinks he's predestined for Heaven, he does. But I wager he's got another think coming.

"Anyway, the wife of the beaten servant was what you might call a 'peculiar woman' and she put a curse on Chosen."

I clapped my hands. "A curse! I love it!"

"'Who treats a man like a dog shall die by a dog,' she said."

"And did he?" I asked.

"Don't rush the story," Laurel chided, wagging a finger. "Chosen had a dog—a black dog—which he abused unmercifully. Over time, the dog, otherwise a naturally pleasant creature, became fearful and then aggressive."

"It turned against Chosen?"

"Yes. It would growl and snarl at Chosen, baring its teeth when the man came close. Eventually, tormented beyond endurance, the dog snapped and attacked him."

"Fatally?"

"Nope. Chosen was a strong man, and he strangled the dog with his bare hands. It wasn't long after that the haunting began."

I sat up straighter. "What form did it take?"

Laurel spoke with relish. "It was said that a phantom black dog prowled the grounds of Hailey House. And the Preston that saw it was destined soon to die."

I leaned back in disappointment. "Black dog legends are quite common." I said.

"Maybe so," Laurel consented, undeterred. "But there's more. Not unexpectedly, Chosen was the first to, ah…"

"Be chosen?" I offered.

"Go," she corrected. "They found him sitting in his chair in his study one morning. Stone-cold dead, the window wide open, and such a look of horror on his face that they had to cover it up before they could move him. The doctor called it 'apoplexy,' but people in the town thought otherwise. Nobody much went to the funeral except for the family and the preacher.

"It was maybe a month later that the oldest son was found expired in the woods. And when the second son met his end a month or so after that—both of them looking like they'd gazed into the pit of Hell—which, who knows, maybe they had—the family decided something had to be done, as there was only the youngest left, and him just a boy. And so—very reluctantly, after the local minister declared himself powerless against the demon dog—they called in a priest to deal with it."

"A priest?" I exclaimed.

"I expect that since the Prestons felt that Catholics were only one step removed from the devil, that evil could combat evil. At any rate, a priest came, and after much exertion was able to contain the phantom dog in a cave in the hills. And there, according to legend, it still lives. Even though it has never been seen again, people say that sometimes when the moon is full, its howls can still be heard."

"Probably just the wind," I said, remembering Chika's cries in the night

"Probably," Laurel said. "But it's a good story anyway, isn't it? More tea?"

I agreed to both story and tea. "So this cave is near the Preston property?"

"That's my understanding," she said, adding with a laugh, "assuming there's some truth behind the legend. But I've never heard of anyone looking for it or trying to open it, and I've lived here all my life."

"Well," I said, setting down my second empty cup and gaining my feet,

"I hope the phantom stays on his side of the boundary wall."

"I don't think you have anything to fear," Laurel said. "Now, if you look over here, I have some books of local history and folklore that might interest you. One even has the story of the Preston's Curse, unless I sold it already…"

Who could resist looking for a cave that contained a captive ghost? Figuring that, except on the days when he circumnavigated his property, Preston probably kept mostly to his house, I began my investigation from the rear of my acreage where it adjoined his. From there, I scrambled up and down the hillside, searching for rocky outcroppings that might indicate the presence of a cave. And always keeping an eye in the direction of Preston's house, just in case.

I spent a whole afternoon, and found…nothing.

That night I heard a dog howling again…my skin crawled before I remembered that it had to be Chika as the full moon—the Hunter's moon—wasn't due for several more days.

My heart ached for the poor creature.

Stubbornness is in my genes, and so I wasn't going to give up after just one afternoon. But it took me three days of intermittent poking around before finally, late one afternoon, I spotted an outcropping with a darker area that might represent an opening. Perhaps it was nothing, as I'd had a number of false alarms before, but I climbed up for a closer look.

I had to push aside a tangle of roots and brush away some moss. But then my heart skipped as I studied the rocks that had been wedged in to block the entrance to what was obviously a small cave. And if I needed further proof, etched into one of them was a faint, weatherworn cross.

I traced it with my finger, then took several photos to document my find.

I briefly considered moving the rocks to see what might be inside…and decided against it. I didn't want to meet a ghost—human or otherwise.

But on the other hand…

Late the following day I was sitting on my porch writing when a shadow fell across my table and I looked up to see Elder Preston standing at the base of the steps, feet planted wide apart, left arm hanging by his side, right one carrying his shotgun, pointing at the ground.

"Have you seen Chika?" he demanded. "She broke her chain and got loose. Hasn't been home since yesterday."

I swallowed, thinking it better not to mention that Chika had surprised me in the act of examining the walled-up cave. I'd nearly fainted when her cold, wet nose had pushed up under the back of my shirt.

But once I'd recovered my poise, we'd sat there for a while, side by side, gazing out over the valley, the hills blanketed in the reds and yellows and oranges of fall. From time to time I'd scratched her between the ears, and she'd replied with a lick on my hand.

She'd wanted to follow me when I left, but I'd told her not to. The thought of Preston showing up with his shotgun had given me the willies. She'd seemed disappointed, and had curled up in a ball as I'd made my way back down the hillside.

And now here he was.

"Not recently," I replied cautiously.

Preston scowled, and shuffled from foot to foot. Beads of sweat dotted his brow, and a muscle twitched in his cheek.

"I spotted her up on the hill," he said, motioning with the shotgun. "She was sniffing around a cave."

"Searching for a den?" I offered.

He glanced back over his shoulder, and then back at me. "She might have been digging. Least ways, there were some stones that looked as though they'd been moved. Too big for a dog, though, I'd have thought…"

His stare was unnerving.

I curled my fingers. *Should have cleaned under my nails…*

"German Shepherds can be strong," I said. "And determined."

He wiped his lip with the back of his left hand.

"She ran off when she saw me coming," he said at last. "Stupid dog. She's going to get the hiding of her life when I get my hands on her. Let me know if you see her."

"I'm going to pick apples in a little while," I said as he turned to walk away, holding the shotgun at the ready. "I'll keep my eyes open."

…arriving back at my house, I set the basket of apples on the kitchen counter and telephoned the sheriff, who didn't sound too excited about coming to Hailey House at night. "We generally leave Mr. Preston alone," he told me. "What he does on his own property is his business."

"But I think there might be something seriously wrong," I said. "He was quite agitated and screaming that something was chasing him."

Grudgingly—after muttering about 'crazy loners' and 'too much to drink'—he agreed to come. He parked his car at the end of the driveway, where I met him, and we walked towards Hailey House together, both of us carrying flashlights.

"You were in your orchard, you say?" he asked, shining his light from side to side, its bright yellow beam contrasting with the silver illumination of the full moon that shafted through the trees, casting a ghostly radiance.

"Yes. It's on the other side of the property wall. Mr. Preston was running through the woods, shooting at something."

"Or someone?"

"'It's after me!' were his words."

"'*It's*.' Not '*he's*'. You're sure?"

"Positive."

"Did you see what it was?"

"No. But he looked terrified."

"Which way was he going?"

"My impression was that he was making for the house," I said, flicking the beam of my flashlight ahead.

Not a glimmer of light shone in the windows of Hailey House, but Chika was there, lying beside the door, licking her paws. She trotted over to me and rubbed against my leg.

The door was shut and locked. The sheriff gave the windows a cursory examination. "No sign of forced entry."

He rang the bell and pounded the knocker.

"Let's go around back," he said, when there was no answer.

We circled the house, and there we found Elder Preston sprawled on the ground, not far from the back door. He lay on his back, his shotgun beside him, one finger still on the trigger. His other arm was extended, the fingers bent like claws as if in a final paroxysm of terror—or as if trying to ward off something. His eyes, wide with horror, bulged in his contorted face. His mouth hung open in a final silent scream.

The sheriff dropped to his haunches.

"Dead," he pronounced, feeling Preston's arched neck. "No obvious sign of violence." He waved the beam from his flashlight over the body. "He might have had a heart attack. Sure looks as though something frightened him to death." He stood up and turned in a circle. "Don't see any tracks, though…"

"'Deliver my life from the power of the dog,'" I whispered, too quietly for the sheriff to hear, adding, "'He shall have judgment without mercy who has shown no mercy.'"

"I'll call the coroner," the sheriff said, finishing his examination of the area.

"Were there any relatives?" I asked. "Anyone to take care of Chika?"

He tapped his flashlight against his leg. "Can't say for sure, but I seem to recall hearing once that he might have been the last of his line. Be up to Animal Control, I suppose."

"I know the dog. If it's all right with you, may I…"

He shrugged. "Fine. One less hassle for me to deal with. I'll clear it with them." He turned aside and moved a few paces away, reaching for his radio.

Chika raised her paw and I stooped over to meet it with my palm.

Then I straightened. And just for an instant, I thought I saw a dark shadow—an ill-defined, dog-shaped *something* with glowing orbs for eyes— sitting in the moonlight, regarding us. My spine tingled before I realized that I felt no malice coming from it…but, perhaps, *satisfaction*.

Then it was gone, and I was left blinking my eyes.

Chika was studying me with her head tilted to one side. She wagged her tail.

"Come, girl," I said, ruffling the soft fur of her head. "There's a new life ahead for you."

twelve

DARK ANGEL

It was mid-afternoon and we had just paused to water the horses from a small brook, when Aznavur, our guide, translator, and overseer, slid from his saddle and approached. His steps were slow, even hesitant, his brow furrowed and lips pursed. He had, I thought, the appearance of a man bearing unwelcome news.

"Yes?" Roger Whittington asked, taking a swallow from his canteen. "What is it?"

Aznavur exhaled loudly, and stared at the dust-stained tips of his boots. "The men are refusing to go any further."

Whittington glared down at the overseer, then swiveled his head towards the half-dozen sullen-looking tribesmen who'd halted their horses some little distance away. "What is the meaning of this?" he demanded.

"My apologies," Aznavur continued, raising his eyes and spreading his hands, "but they say that they are Christian men and will not go into that valley."

Whittington's face reddened. "You told me they'd be reliable! I'm paying them good money—"

"They say it is not enough to enter the home of Mug Hreshtaky," Aznavur said, the Armenian words sounding ominous. He made the sign of the Cross over his chest.

"Just my luck to hire a bunch of superstitious peasants," Whittington muttered through clenched teeth. He reached for the rifle slung over his shoulder. "Perhaps this will encourage them."

I held out a hand to forestall his movement.

"Don't be silly, Roger," I said, earning my own glare from Whittington and an appreciative glance from Aznavur.

"In fact," I added, "I can't say as I blame them." For it was indeed a gloomy panorama that lay before us. Rugged, barren mountains lumped on either side, while ahead of us a brown and gray wasteland of high desert meandered into a narrow valley whose end lay out of sight. It was no different from several other valleys we had encountered on our trek through the mountains of Armenia, but for some reason, although I don't consider myself to be either a nervous or imaginative man, it gave me the willies, and I almost wished I hadn't taken up Roger Whittington's offer to accompany his expedition as photographer.

"What are your plans for the summer?" he'd asked one day, finding me morosely studying the River Wear flow beneath the imposing edifice of Durham Cathedral. "Do you still have any?"

I shook my head. "Not any longer," I replied, as visions of my planned wedding and honeymoon subsided into the dark waters of disappointment.

"Don't worry," he said, his jocular tone grating. "There are plenty of girls in the world. A better one will come along. You'll see."

He was probably right. After all, the girl to whom I'd been engaged had, she said, found a more desirable match than I presented. So why shouldn't the same happen to me? Still, I wasn't in the mood to appreciate Whittington's ham-handed effort at consolation.

"Do you have something in mind?" I asked.

156

"Yes," he replied, dropping to sit beside me on the bench, and pulling off his glasses to polish them. "Come to Armenia with me."

"Armenia?" I laughed, despite myself. "If it was the French Riviera, or Corfu, or Mallorca, maybe. But Armenia?"

"I need a photographer," he said, replacing his glasses, "and you need a change of scenery."

"I don't know," I said.

"It's a once in a lifetime opportunity," he insisted. "I managed to obtain special permission from the Soviet Ministry for Culture—favour from an old colleague. Mind you, it might be a bit primitive—horses, and all that."

"Thanks for the offer." I didn't find the idea of bouncing around on horseback in the middle of nowhere to be terribly appealing. "But no."

"Miranda Cooke is coming," Whittington added, almost casually, his gaze fixed across the river.

"Miranda?" I exclaimed. "You're joking!"

"She's going to be the official project historian." He gave me a wink.

I scoffed, "She's never looked twice at me."

"That's not exactly true, and you know it. Even if it was, Derek, I think I know my cousin better than you do." He lowered his voice. "I shouldn't tell you this, but she's the one who suggested I invite you."

"I sincerely doubt it," I said coldly.

He shrugged and rose to his feet. "Suit yourself. If you'd prefer to stay here and spend your summer in a funk rather than getting some professional exposure on what promises to be an exciting dig in the company of a beautiful woman, so be it."

He turned away.

"What do you hope to discover?" I asked.

He halted and swung back around. "An ancient temple complex, I believe."

I snorted. "I should have known."

"I found a reference to it in an obscure volume in the library of a defunct monastery—"

I cut him off. "You're sure that Miranda is coming."

"Positive."

I came to a decision. "All right. You can count me in."

He clapped me on the shoulder. "That's the spirit! We leave in a fortnight."

"That's not much time!" I protested.

"More than enough!" And with that, he left me.

Now, here we were in the lonely wilderness of the Armenian mountains, rugged places where vehicles couldn't go—not exactly a prepossessing place in which to site a religious complex, I would have thought. I suppose there was a certain stark beauty about it, but had it not been for Miranda's presence, I fear that it would have deepened my mood of despondency.

"I'm not about to be thwarted having come this far," Whittington gritted, removing his hand from his rifle. "But it will be a lot of work if it's just the three of us digging."

"Let me handle it," Miranda said from his far side. She swung lithely to the ground, took Aznavur's arm, and drew him aside. They talked together for a few minutes, Miranda quite earnestly, Aznavur in a more restrained manner. Then Miranda remounted her horse, while Aznavur addressed his men in Armenian.

Gradually the scowls changed to grudging nods.

"The men will come," Aznavur said, returning to us.

"Excellent!" Whittington beamed. "Then let's continue!"

We urged the horses on towards the valley.

"What did you say to make them come?" Whittington asked.

Miranda gave him a charming smile—one that I wish had been directed at me. "It was a combination of factors. I told them I was disappointed that they were afraid to go where a woman dared to venture."

"Appealing to the primitive male ego?" Whittington queried.

"More like hitting them in it," I said.

She touched the crucifix which dangled from her necklace. "I said we should rely on Heaven for protection—yes, Roger, I know you disparage my views, but some of us do have faith."

"Listen to the lady, Roger," I added in agreement.

"And what else?" Whittington asked suspiciously.

"I promised them double pay," Miranda concluded.

Whittington nearly fell off his horse.

"It's better than going home empty handed," she pointed out as he struggled for speech.

"She's got you there, old boy," I said, giving Miranda a salute.

He groused for the next couple of miles, but we paid no heed, and he eventually lapsed into silence.

We made camp that night at the entrance to the valley. The men still seemed nervous, but with Aznavur's help, Miranda encouraged them into singing a round of folk songs, and that lightened the mood. I would have liked to say that I slept well, but I tossed and turned and awoke stiff and sore by the time dawn arrived.

Not that morning was much of anything. The sky was weighed down by masses of dull, grey cloud, and a strong wind buffeted us, as if trying to keep us from proceeding down the valley. My sense of unease intensified, nurtured, no doubt, by the awesome silence which seemed to speak of a great loneliness—or great dread. I shivered, and kept sneaking glances at Miranda to see how she was responding.

We trekked through the morning, the mountains on either side gradually becoming lower as the valley wound between them. The wind died away and the clouds thinned, but still obscured the sun. Eventually, around noon, we rounded a bend—and halted in amazement.

The mountains, by now no more than hills, came to an abrupt end, leaving the valley floor projecting out like a short, rounded tongue over a vast plain which lay some hundred feet below. The scene would have been awe-inspiring enough, but what took our breath away was a huge basin—a natural amphitheater near the tip of the tongue—and on the far side—

"Mug Hreshtaky," Aznavur whispered from behind me.

A monolith of black stone perhaps sixty feet tall reared up from the edge of the cliff. It was surely natural, yet it could not have been more deliberately set for dramatic purpose.

"It's amazing," Miranda said, sliding to the ground and standing on the lip of the amphitheater. I moved to join her, in my mind already assessing the vantage points for the pictures I would take.

"An astounding location for a religious site," Whittington said rapturously, running his eyes over the rubble-strewn ground. "I want you to take detailed photographs, Derek, and then we'll decide where to start our first dig—"

Behind us, the tribesmen murmured—and it took no translation to discern that their fears were still threatening to get the better of them. Whittington seemed oblivious to their agitation.

"You'd better reassure the men, first," I replied, indicating them with a wave of my hand.

Whittington cast them a scornful glance, then strode around the amphitheater to the base of the monolith. He gave it a resounding slap.

"It's a rock," he called back. "That's all it is. A big rock." He slapped it again.

Aznavur grinned and said something to his companions. The grumbling subsided.

"Set up camp," Whittington ordered, returning, and Aznavur chivvied the workers into action.

I strolled up to the monolith.

"What are you thinking?" Miranda asked, following me, while Whittington went to point out where he wanted the tents erecting.

"There's something wrong here, Miranda," I mused, scanning the monolith—the Dark Angel—for signs of human workmanship, and finding none.

She nodded slowly, and to my surprise said, "I feel something too— like an aura. What do you suppose went on here, Derek?"

I shook my head. "I don't know. And I'm not sure that I want to." I motioned in Whittington's direction. "But *he* does. It's strange how a man who doesn't believe in the supernatural is so intrigued by ancient religious sites."

Her forehead wrinkled. "A lot of it is just fascination with ancient peoples. And I'm not sure what he does or doesn't believe. Sometimes his skepticism seems genuine, at other times strained—as if he can't shake off the suspicion that there might be something real underlying religious belief."

I puffed out my cheeks. "Still, it's just a big rock." I forced myself to smile. "I'd best see that the crew isn't being too rough with my equipment."

While some of the men unloaded gear and supplies, others set up a trio of tents for me, Miranda, and Whittington, and then a cluster some distance apart for themselves.

As soon as my equipment was safely unpacked, I busied myself taking a series of preliminary images. Whittington stalked over the site, muttering to himself and drawing lines and angles in the air with his hands. Miranda perched on a stool outside her tent and wrote in her journal.

As I worked, my sense of unease gradually faded and I actually began to feel as if the expedition might possibly be good for me. It would certainly help me professionally, and since my personal life lay in ruins, that was no small thing.

But it was as the sun was sagging listlessly towards the violet-tinted horizon that another unpleasant sensation occurred. The plateau—which is what the valley floor had become—was oriented east to west, with the monolith on the eastern end. We had finished eating and were preparing to retire early, since Whittingon was eager to begin digging as soon as it was light enough in the morning.

The sun slid behind the hills. A shadow crept over the ground and enveloped the monolith even as a shaft of light faded.

For a moment it was as if I were witnessing a bizarre transformation. The monolith was no longer a massive pillar of rock but a giant figure. Its cowled head was downcast, obscuring its face except for a line of cruel lips. Its wings were folded behind its back, and its arms were crossed over its chest. It was great, brooding, and menacing—an angel of darkness. I wanted to tear my eyes away, grab my camera for a shot, but I couldn't move.

"Derek! Derek!"

Miranda's voice broke the spell, and I looked over to where she'd been doing some stretches outside her tent.

"Are you all right?" she asked.

"Fine," I said, giving what was probably a nervous-sounding laugh. I glanced back at the monolith, but the effect was already fading, and in seconds had vanished.

"Did you see the monolith? It looked weird in the light."

"Yes," she replied. "Perhaps that's how it got its name."

"Could be."

"The effect is called pareidolia," she expanded. "Seeing figures and faces in things."

"Like animals in clouds."

"Exactly."

I accepted her explanation, albeit reluctantly, and went to bed with the disturbing image still in my mind. Yet I slept well, and when I rose to find sunlight splashing golden over the plateau, all my previous disquiet vanished.

Aznavur had organized his men into teams, and they began excavating in the locations Whittington had decided upon. Having little to do until any artifacts were unearthed, I amused myself by taking artistic shots of the scenery, such as might enhance any prose work that Miranda produced. It wasn't long, however, before Whittington hailed me.

"Look at this, Derek," he said, indicating a row of stone blocks and what was obviously part of a fallen column. "The foundation of a temple, I should imagine."

I hastened to photograph the find from various angles.

"I expect there'll be an altar around here somewhere," Whittington added.

"I wonder what they sacrificed?" I queried.

"Too early to tell," he said, shaking his head. "If we're lucky we might find some animal bones or ritual objects."

"I haven't seen many animals around here," I countered, sweeping my arm in a circle.

"No, but back then they were quite likely more plentiful," he said.

The workers made steady progress, and the trenches widened and deepened, and Whittington scurried everywhere like a panic-stricken beetle, trying to watch everyone and everything. I kept an eye on the monolith and a camera ready in case the trick of light reoccurred, but either the light wasn't right or my viewing angle was wrong, as nothing happened.

"Roger's certainly in his element," I remarked to Miranda later as we sat on campstools beside a flickering fire after the day's work had ended.

"When he's on a project, there's no slowing him down," Miranda said, brushing back a strand of fair hair from her high forehead.

"Was he like that as a child?"

"Always. Flitting from one activity to another, digging in the back yard in search of buried treasure..." She laughed. "I knew that whenever there was a family gathering I'd be swept up into his latest fantasy."

"Were you ever..." I began cautiously, letting the sentence trail off.

She looked at me for a long moment until she caught my meaning. I couldn't help but be almost mesmerized by her lustrous blue eyes, and the auburn shimmer of her hair, lit by the dancing firelight.

"Never!" she chuckled. "We're poles apart."

"You're interested in archaeology..."

"Yes, but only as a subject for writing. Not as an all-consuming passion." She allowed her gaze to return to the fire. "And philosophically— or should I say religiously—we're miles apart, also."

She stirred the ground with her foot. "I'm glad you're here, Derek. I feel as if I have an ally...I shouldn't like to be in this place with only Roger."

Despite the chill of the night, I felt warm inside.

"He said that you'd suggested I come along," I said.

I thought her cheeks pinked slightly. "It sounds silly, Derek, but I had this feeling..."

"A premonition?"

"Perhaps. Roger mocked me. But I felt that you would take me seriously..."

"I do," I said, reaching over to lay my hand on top of hers. "I do indeed."

She grimaced. "We sound like a couple of children."

"Not at all, Miranda," I said. "Not at all."

We sat in silence for a few minutes, then she rose. "See you in the morning, Derek."

"Sleep well," I replied.

I stayed up for a while longer, watching the fire die down, and thinking how strange life could be.

The next several days passed without incident. The diggers uncovered additional ruins, and also began to unearth some more interesting items—pottery cups and bowls, bronze figurines, knives, curious vessels which Whittington said were for burning incense, coins, jewelry, inscriptions…each of which I dutifully photographed *in situ*, and then again once removed and cleaned. Miranda recorded everything, and we conversed for hours, on both professional and personal topics.

Despite the fact that the expedition had settled into a routine—and nothing untoward had occurred—neither of us was able to shake a sensation of lingering unease. We developed the habit of praying together before retiring, much to Whittington's amusement.

It was some ten days after our arrival that a shout from Whittington alerted me that an exceptional discovery had been made. I abandoned the catalogue of photographs on which I'd been working and hurried over, Miranda beside me.

Whittington was fairly dancing in ecstasy.

"Look at this! Look at this!" he exclaimed.

We looked.

It was a slab of stone some ten feet long, six feet wide, and a foot thick. The sides were tan in color, flecked with gold and silver. It could have been any kind of rock for all I knew—but my stomach knotted as the workmen brushed dirt away, revealing a surface marred by ugly, reddish-brown patches.

"What is it?" I asked.

"The altar!" Whittington proclaimed. He bent over to point. "And see here…there's an inscription running all the way around." He beckoned to Miranda. "Sketch it for me, please."

He straightened, rubbing his hands together. "Now we'll learn something, if I can translate that."

"Are we sure that we want to?" I muttered, barely loud enough for Miranda to hear, and she glanced up at me, before returning her attention to her notebook.

Whittington snapped his fingers. "What are you standing around for, Derek? Photographs!"

I hastened to comply.

We worked until the light was fading and Whittington called a halt for the day.

"Could you make anything of the inscription?" I asked Miranda.

"Nothing," she replied, nodding to where a light burned in Whittington's tent. "We'll have to see if Roger can figure it out. He's not likely to rest until he does."

"Take a walk with me?" I asked.

"Love it," she said. "Where to?"

"Nowhere in particular...just away."

The truth was that I felt like escaping, even for a little while, the presence of the brooding monolith and the sacrificial altar.

I took her hand, picked up a torch, and together we skirted the workmen's camp and ambled up the valley. Stars shone in a black-velvet sky, and a waning crescent moon hovered above the hills.

"Is something the matter?" Miranda asked.

"I'm just restless tonight," I replied. "Seeing that altar..."

"It gave me the creeps, too."

"I'll be glad when this over and we can return to England, and normalcy. Although..."

"Although what?" her eyes glimmered like stars themselves.

"If it means being parted from you..."

"Who says that it does?" She halted and drew closer to me.

I sighed. "This isn't real life, Miranda. This is an interlude. Once we're back in England, I'll just be plain old Derek, and you—"

"What about me?"

"You'll be on to better things."

A sharp note entered her voice. "What is that supposed to mean?"

"Only...only that you're too good for the likes of me."

She pushed back and looked up at me. "Don't be ridiculous, Derek. I've thought for a long time that you...that you were someone I could imagine myself falling for."

"Seriously?" I gasped. "I never guessed—"

"I could hardly bear to see you becoming involved with a girl who wasn't worth your time. In fact, I was heartily glad to hear that she'd jilted you."

"Miranda, I—"

"Your problem, Derek Bancroft," she said, jabbing a finger to my chest, "is that you have too low an opinion of yourself. If you could step back and look at yourself, you'd see someone quite different."

I didn't know what to say. We stood there in the moon-dappled landscape simply enjoying each other's presence.

A cool breeze drifted down from the hills. "We'd best be heading back," I said, putting an arm around Miranda's shoulders.

We parted at the entrance to her tent.

"Think about what I said, Derek," she enjoined as I bid her good night.

I should have slept well in the glow of the knowledge of Miranda's affection, but I didn't. Instead, to my dismay, I dreamed of the altar which Whittington had unearthed. I saw it as perhaps it had once appeared hundreds—or thousands—of years ago.

In my dream it rested upon a massive pedestal, surrounded by columns. The amphitheater was filled with a host of indistinguishable human figures. It was night—a dark, moonless night—and shadows danced and flitted in the light of countless flaming torches. Flutes, drums, cymbals, and human voices combined into a chorus of throbbing beats and undulating melody that wrapped around the towering monolith before radiating into the desolate landscape.

A robed figure stood behind the altar, a blade glittering in its hand. Two other figures emerged from the shadows, dragging a third—a woman, her hands and feet bound. Together, they hoisted her and laid her upon the altar. The chorus rose to a deafening pitch, then stopped. Into the silence, the priest intoned an incantation.

And the monolith—it was as if the wings unfurled, the arms extended, and the giant figure leaned forward in expectation.

The knife flashed.

The priest held a cup to catch flowing blood, which he presented to the looming figure.

The attendants raised the limp body, and cast it over the precipice—

And I awoke, clammy, with my heart racing and hands and feet tingling. Shaking, I stepped out of my tent into the cool of the night air until the sweat dried on my skin and I reached for a blanket. And there I stayed until dawn crested over the horizon.

"You look rough," Miranda commented, as I picked at my breakfast of bacon and beans.

She, I noticed, looked as fresh as ever.

"A bad dream," I replied, wondering if it had really been a dream or a true vision of the past.

Whittington handed me a cup of coffee. "See if this helps."

I sipped it slowly, never having enjoyed coffee, but a semblance of life crept back into me. "I'd like to explore the base of the cliffs," I said, and both of them looked at me in surprise.

"Whatever for?" Whittington asked.

"You've found an altar," I replied, "but have you found any remains?"

He shook his head. "Not a one. Which would be unusual if the animals were then consumed on site, as one would expect."

"Is it safe, Derek?" Miranda wondered. "Is there a path?"

"I can rappel down," I said. "I have plenty of experience."

"Aznavur can help you," Whittington said.

"As will I," Miranda added.

It didn't take long to collect an adequate length of rope, belayed and secured to a boulder, and to fashion a harness.

"Do you really expect to find anything?" Miranda said, as I stood on the brink, with a shovel slung over my shoulder, and a small pack on my back.

"I hope not," I said, motioning to Aznavur to begin paying out rope.

I made my way down the cliff face, from time to time looking up to see Aznavur and Miranda watching anxiously. Upon reaching the bottom, I unhooked the harness, and studied the scree.

"Anything?" Miranda called down.

"Nothing on the surface," I shouted back.

I chose a spot directly below the monolith and began to dig. Fortunately the scree was loose, and I made good progress. I dug for a while, but found nothing. I then moved some feet to my left and tried again.

I had gone down about four feet and was about to give up, when a flash of white caught my attention. I cast my shovel aside and bent over to remove the remainder of the dirt with my hands.

"What did you find?" Miranda called.

I straightened and held up my discovery. "What I hoped not to."

She put her hand over her mouth, and Aznavur crossed himself at the sight of the human skull I held.

I put the skull in my pack, and resumed digging. In a few minutes I had uncovered another skull and a collection of various disarticulated bones.

"Help me up," I called to Aznavur, and began my ascent.

"This is truly an accursed place," Aznavur said, when once I had reached the top and unbuckled myself.

"Aznavur's right," I said to Miranda. "It's as if the whole area has been saturated by evil."

"Roger feels nothing of it," Miranda said as we walked back to our tents. "He's totally oblivious."

"If only we could convince him to leave."

"It would be futile," she said. "He planned two months for this dig. He won't quit before then."

Whittington was enthusiastic when he saw the skulls. "A human sacrificial cult!" he exclaimed, turning one of the skulls over in his hands. "Who would have guessed?"

"Wasn't Armenia the first country to officially become Christian?" I asked.

"Yes," he said, pausing in his examination of the skull. "The Kingdom of Armenia adopted Christianity in 301 under Tiridates III."

"So is this site earlier or later?"

"The cult, I expect, predates that," Whittington said. "And perhaps the advent of Christianity is why this remote site was chosen to continue what would certainly have been forbidden rites."

He set the skulls on a table outside his tent. "You've been a great help, Derek. Thanks to your intuition—"

I waved the compliment aside. Because I didn't feel complimented. I felt sick.

I spent the afternoon puttering around the dig site, disturbed by the connection of my dream to reality. The men, I could tell, were upset, news of my discovery obviously having circulated.

"I don't know how much longer they will stay," Aznavur confided in me. "They are afraid...they say they have been here long enough, and it will only tempt fate to remain."

"I doubt that I can do much," I replied, "but I'll try to talk to Dr. Whittington."

But Whittington would hear none of it, dismissing me curtly for interrupting his work on the inscription. "The find of the century, and you want to leave?" he scowled, not looking up from his table.

"I told you," Miranda said as I sat morosely outside my tent.

"If only he'd get sick...break a leg...give us some excuse to return to civilization."

"Derek!" she exclaimed.

I waved a hand. "Oh, I don't wish any serious harm to him. It's this place. I'm sorry."

The sun had set and stars were showing when Whittington emerged from his tent waving a piece of paper. "I've done it! Deciphered the inscription!"

"What does it say?" Miranda asked.

Whittington adopted a lecturing tone. "Armenian script wasn't developed until 405 for a translation of the Bible. Before then, they used Aramaic and Greek. At first I thought it might be Aramaic, but then I realized it was Pahlavi."

"What's that?" I wondered.

"Parthian," he explained. "Developed around 250 BC and derived from Aramaic. I'm not an expert, but I have a basic knowledge of Parthian."

"So what does it say?" Miranda repeated.

"It's fascinating! Absolutely unique!"

"Don't keep us in suspense!"

Whittington beckoned. "Over here."

He picked up a torch and led us across the ground to the excavated altar. I noticed Aznavur and several of the men watching us from a distance.

Whittington fluttered the paper. "I expected it to be a dedication—along the lines of 'erected to the god or goddess so and so by king such and such in thanks for victory or whatever'. But it's not. It's an invocation. An incantation if you will."

A cold chill crept up my spine. It suddenly dawned on me that it was the night of the new moon.

"Roger...don't," I said.

He stared at me in amazement—a look which rapidly became scornful.

"Don't tell me you're afraid of some ancient gibberish, Derek," he scoffed.

"Just let us read it," I urged. "Don't speak the words."

"I can't believe this!" Whittington exclaimed. "You've been spending too much time with the tribesmen. They've infected you with their superstitions."

"I agree with Derek," Miranda said, shooting me a worried look. "Please, Roger, leave it alone."

"You two are really something," Whittington retorted. Suddenly, he laughed. "You're pulling my leg, aren't you? Having a joke at my expense."

"Not at all," I said.

His amused expression faded. "Well, I'm not pandering to your foolishness."

He raised the paper. I lunged for it, but anticipating my movement, Whittington was quicker. He yanked it away, then, with more agility than I thought he possessed, jumped up on the altar.

"No you don't, Derek," he said, keeping out of arms' reach.

"Roger, for pity's sake—"

He assumed a pose as if her were an orator and shone the torchlight on the paper. "I'll read it in Parthian first. Pardon my accent. I don't know the correct pronunciation." He began to intone.

I couldn't reproduce, even if I wanted to, the sound of the words that he uttered. They were weird, uncanny, especially in that place, with the monolith looming over us and the slab of the altar in front of us. It was as if they emanated from some other world, coming through a portal that should never be opened.

I gripped the edge of the altar. Miranda was breathing rapidly beside me.

Whittington finished and for a moment a dense silence prevailed. "That wasn't so bad, was it?" he said. "Here's the English translation. 'Come, dire Lord of Night...'"

I lost track of his words.

For Miranda had stopped breathing. She was staring past Whittington, her face a mask of dread. I followed her gaze, and my own breath halted. A black tide of horror threatened to overwhelm me.

Because the monolith was bending, the hooded figure leaning forwards, just as I had seen in my dream! My heart lurched as the giant wings unfurled. Then its head tipped back to reveal a pair of eyes burning red with hellfire. A sensation washed over me, as of hunger—a hunger that had been long unsatisfied, growing and festering for century on century—.

A choking sound came from Miranda's throat. Or maybe it was mine.

I was barely aware of Whittington's voice ceasing, and him regarding us in perplexity, before slowly turning to face the monolith.

And then the ground shook and the air vibrated with a noise as of rolling thunder—or like some deep, awful laughter. Someone yelled—it might have been Whittington or Aznavur—and then a hailstorm of small rocks rained down, skittering across the ground and pouring over the precipice into the valley below.

I struggled against the altar to maintain my balance. With a shriek, Miranda fell and slid away.

"Oh God, not Miranda!" I cried, and flung myself after her, straining to reach her. Our fingers touched and I clutched her hand, spread-eagling myself and clawing at any irregularity in the rock to slow us down.

The ground steadied, and I took the opportunity to haul her towards me. I scrambled to my feet, yanking her up, then hand in hand we ran even as the ground bucked again and another deluge of stone pelted down. We rounded the amphitheater, then dodged and weaved through a pandemonium of shouting men and neighing, rearing horses. Miranda stumbled over some rubble and would have fallen, but I scooped her into my arms and staggered on.

I suppose I should have been afraid, but I wasn't. My mind seemed crystal clear. I heard Miranda gasping a prayer, and into my thoughts came a verse from one of the Psalms—"You will not fear the terror of the night."

The tents were just ahead of us. Then the ground heaved as if it would launch us into the night sky. I lost my grip and Miranda dropped from my arms. I came down heavily, then rolled to cover her with my body as a panicked horse clattered past.

I twisted to look back to where the monolith should have been, but as I did so, a giant black wing blotted out the stars overhead and enveloped me. A deafening crack sounded from beside me. Pain exploded through my head, and I knew no more.

When I came to, I found myself lying on the ground with a cushion under my head and the rosy glow of dawn overhead.

I must have groaned as I sat up, because in an instant Miranda was kneeling beside me. Her face—smeared with dirt, but still beautiful—a picture of concern.

"Derek! Are you all right?"

"I think so," I said. "Bruised and sore, and with a splitting headache, but otherwise intact. How about you?"

"A few scuff marks is all."

"Help me up, would you?"

She gripped my arm as I struggled to my feet, wincing as various muscles protested, and blinking at a transient wave of dizziness.

"What a mess," I said. Around me the camp lay in a shambles of collapsed tents—including the one that must have fallen on me in the night—broken poles and packing cases, and debris. One of the hillsides showed a raw wound, the source of the avalanche.

It took a moment for the silence to register and for me to realize that we were alone.

"Where is everyone?" I asked.

"They took off as soon as it was daylight," Miranda replied. "Mug Hreshtaky had spoken, and they weren't staying a moment longer. They left us a pair of horses and some supplies."

I stared at her, speechless for a long minute. "Aznavur wouldn't have—!"

"He wanted to take us along, but I didn't think it was safe to move you. And I wouldn't leave without Roger."

"Roger? What's the matter with him?"

Her shoulders rose. "No one has seen him, since the earthquake hit."

I pivoted to face the monolith, afraid of what I might see, and half expecting it to be gone, toppled by the earthquake. But there it stood, seemingly unchanged, towering above the amphitheater and the blood-colored altar.

"It *was* just an earthquake, wasn't it?" I said slowly, hoping that the blow on my head had addled my brains and that I hadn't really seen what I thought I'd seen...and yet I remembered the horrified expression on Miranda's face when Whittington finished his incantation. I could have doubted my own sanity, but not hers as well. Unless we had both been the victims of some bizarre hallucination-

Her eyes clouded as she searched mine. She bit her lip, made a slight sideways movement of her head.

"I wish it had been," she whispered.

"Well," I said, trying to sound confident, "at least we're alive to tell."

She gave a slight smile. "Thanks to you," she said, resting a hand on my shoulder and squeezing. "I don't know how you did it."

I felt my face grow hot. I took a deep breath. "Let's look for Roger. He could be lying injured somewhere."

She nodded, then hesitated. "Do you think it's safe?"

"I don't think it will come back," I said cautiously, silently praying that I was right. "Unless someone summons it. But there's a possibility of aftershocks."

And so for a week we searched, having moved our tents down the valley and out of sight of the monolith, as neither of us wanted to be near it any more than necessary. We sifted through the entire camp, examining every square inch of the archaeological site, poking through fallen rubble, climbing the hills, shouting his name and hoping to see his figure coming towards us. I rappelled down to the base of the cliffs in case he'd been swept over the precipice, but found nothing.

We searched, even as hope faded, and we retraced ground we'd covered before.

Eventually, as our provisions had dwindled to the point where they were barely adequate to see us back to civilization, we admitted defeat and made the decision to leave. We left food and a note in case Whittington returned. Then we loaded such supplies as we could manage onto the horses, including Miranda's journals, Whittington's field notes, my photographs, and a few easily-portable artifacts, and set off for the long trek back, with a grilling from suspicious Soviet authorities waiting for us.

But before we were out of sight of that dreadful place for the final time, I paused to take one last photograph of the monolith as a wayward shaft of sunlight played across its shrouded form. I don't know why I did it. And it was months before I developed that photograph, by which time Miranda and I were just returned from a honeymoon in Venice.

I never showed it to her.

Perhaps it was only a case of pareidolia, or a trick of the lighting creating a chiaroscuro effect.

That's what I told myself to believe, as it would have been too awful to comprehend otherwise, and my mind balked at what my eyes were telling me.

For, as it had on that first day, the monolith appeared to have transformed. But now, a grim smile crossed the lips of that downcast, hooded face. And embraced in the Dark Angel's folded arms I could clearly discern the twisted body of a man.

thirteen

THE FIFTH DOOR

"It used to stand right here," Cecilia Stark said, stopping beside a streetlight and gesturing with a long, elegant hand festooned with rings glittering with large imitation gems. "Hard to imagine, isn't it?"

I studied the block of flats—typical, uninspired urban architecture, with rows of blank square windows set in featureless brick walls—and nodded.

"There used to be a big oak tree right there," she continued, pointing to a parking area occupied by several road-weary cars and a handful of scooters. "And masses of rhododendrons."

"It must have been beautiful," I said, taking in the weed-dotted walkways, a few dying shrubs, and the forlorn stumps of a couple of trees.

She sighed, and her somewhat square face assumed a faraway expression. "It was, Arielle, it was."

"What did the house look like?" I wondered.

Her pale green eyes appeared to unfocus—a characteristic that I had noticed before and that I found vaguely disturbing, as was her voice, which became almost dreamy.

"It was like…like something out of a gothic story," she said. "Big, and rambling, with room on room, added onto willy-nilly over the centuries without any thought for plan or practicality. It had three stories, with gables, a turret on the left, and a high, pitched roof. There were long corridors, all sorts of nooks and crannies, and fireplaces that you could roast an ox in."

I chuckled. "A cross between a castle and a labyrinth?"

"That's how it seemed to Colin and me."

"Let's sit down," I said, motioning towards a bench missing a slat a few yards away. Cecilia moved in a languid way and perched on the edge, adjusting one of the long, patterned skirts which she fancied, while I leaned back and stretched out my leg, which had begun to ache abominably. It was that leg—or—rather, the injury to it, which had occasioned my first meeting with Cecilia.

I'd been riding my bicycle along the high street when a passing car had clipped me, precipitating me onto the curb with my right leg folded at a highly unanatomical angle. Hearing my cry, a young woman had run out of a grocer's shop and provided comfort and such assistance as she could until the ambulance arrived and carted me away.

Following a stay in the hospital, during which the surgeons implanted the contents of a hardware store in my leg, I'd returned to the shop—having learned that it was owned by her father—to express my thanks for her aid. A friendship of sorts had developed, and one day Cecilia asked if I'd like to see the site of her childhood home. Naturally, I agreed, especially as Cecilia hinted that there had been something mysterious about it, and I was always interested in the mysterious.

"Yes," she said, "Colin and I had many experiences in Carlsfield Manor. It was on the edge of town then, before all this new development sprang up."

She made it sound as if it was long ago, but since she was about my own age of twenty, it was more a reflection of the speed of what is popularly if inaccurately called progress than the passage of time.

"Colin was four years older than I," she continued, "and like most brothers and sisters we had our ups and downs. He could be quite insufferable at times."

"How so?" I asked, and she made a vague gesture.

"You know…ahead of me in school…Mr. Smartypants…stronger, smarter…It didn't help that he was the favourite. Father had always wanted a son, while I was an afterthought."

"It must have been difficult," I sympathized, although being an only child, I couldn't really relate.

"It was," she said. "Because of some neighborhood bullies, we spent most of our free time together, in the house—and that wasn't as confining as it sounds. There was much to explore—rooms filled with the bric-a-brac of centuries, many of which hadn't been entered in decades. With just our parents and the two of us, we only lived in a small part of the house."

She paused to watch a sparrow searching for crumbs.

"The Starks had once been prosperous," she resumed, "but by the time my father inherited Carlsfield Manor—rather unexpectedly from a distant cousin whom we never knew—there wasn't much left. The house had fallen into disrepair, and the only reason Father kept it was because of a sense of family obligation. You can't just dispose of something that has been in the family for centuries, you know. But he struggled to make ends meet. Of course, Colin and I knew nothing of that; we simply thought of the house as our playground."

She spread her hands as if to frame the scene. "Can you imagine a gusty night, the rhododendrons rustling against the windowpanes, the oak tree creaking, and a full moon casting eerie shadows down the halls?"

I nodded. "It sounds creepy."

"Colin was fifteen and I was eleven at the time. One night, having been allowed to stay up much later than usual while our parents entertained guests, we were playing hide and seek in the west wing—a place we rarely ventured. Colin had just found me, and we were walking back along the hallway when he suddenly stopped, and stared at a door, then back along the corridor, then back at the door.

"'Aren't there only four rooms on this side, Cissy?' he asked.

"I nodded. 'Yes.'

"'Well, now there are five.'

"I thought at first he was teasing me, but I looked along the corridor and counted. There were five.

"'Could we have missed one before?' I wondered. He gave me a scornful look.

"'Look at the paint,' he said.

"The doors had once been white, but over the time the paint had peeled, and hung from the wood in long strips. All except that on the middle one, which looked as if it had received a fresh coat.

"Colin went up to it, rattled the knob and shook it.

"'Locked,' he said. He tried to peer through the keyhole. 'It's too dark.'

"I had crept up beside him, and put my ear to the door—don't ask me why. I jerked it away.

"'Listen, Colin,' I said.

"He did as I suggested. Then, his eyes wide, he asked, 'What did you hear?'

"'Screaming,' I said. 'Faint screaming.'

"We looked at each other for a moment, and then we ran."

Cecilia broke off as a motorcycle roared by, and I shifted my weight onto the opposite hip, wishing I had brought a pain pill with me.

"Maybe it was the wind in the chimney," I offered.

"That's what I suggested to Colin when we got downstairs," Cecilia said. "And he agreed. But I don't think either one of us really believed it.

"'What have you two been up to?' Mother asked when she saw us. 'You're pale as ghosts.'

"'Just playing,' we replied. She regarded us suspiciously, but let it go and sent us off to bed.

"We didn't dare go back there that night, but the next day, when the sun was shining, Colin encouraged me to make our way back upstairs. I think he was embarrassed about being afraid. We counted the doors. One, two, three, and four.

"'I was sure there were five,' Colin said, frowning.

"'So was I,' I agreed. All four doors were unlocked, and we opened them, but saw nothing unusual. Colin thought it was strange, but I thought it was positively weird."

"I would have, too," I said.

"Well, we went back up the next day and the next, and always we saw four doors. So we forget about it—at least, I did. But about a month later, Colin knocked on my bedroom door one night, after our parents had gone to bed.

"'Come on,' he said, in a conspiratorial manner.

"'Where to?' I asked.

"'Upstairs,' he whispered, pointing with an index finger.

"'Why?'

"'It's the full moon.'

"I climbed out of bed, put on my slippers, and followed him. Colin had a flashlight, and so we crept into the west wing and up the creaking stairs. I don't know about Colin's, but my heart was racing.

"'Let's count together,' Colin said, shining the light on each door as we passed it, and quietly chanting each number.

"'Five,' I whispered as we reached the last one. 'Colin—let's go back downstairs,'—for now I was scared. I clutched my dressing gown tight around me.

"Colin, however, seemed more curious than afraid.

"'Let's check them out,' he whispered back. Trembling, I followed as he opened the first and second doors, to find rooms filled with dusty furniture and junk, just as before. But the middle door didn't budge. The last two were the same as the first two. We returned to the middle one, pressed our ears to the boards, and again heard the sound of distant screams, perhaps slightly louder than before.

"'There's no wind tonight,' I said, shivering.

"'What could it be?' Colin wondered. 'A bird in the chimney?'

"'I don't want to know,' I said.

"'But I do.' He tapped his finger on the knob. 'Where there's a lock, there must be a key.'

"'So go find it, smarty,' I challenged him.

"'I intend to,' he replied firmly.

"And with that, we returned to our bedrooms.

"The next day, after school, Colin began his search—and convinced me to help, while keeping our quest secret from our parents. Together we went through every room of that rambling old house—looking in closets and cupboards, opening desks and writing tables, poking around in dark corners and cobwebby cellars, rummaging in musty trunks and cases.

"We found a treasure trove of old books, dolls and toys, trinkets and clothes, jewelry and watches—enough to stock an antique store. For days we searched, and while we found quite a few old keys, none of them appeared likely to fit the mysterious door.

"'What have you been up to?' Mother asked when I appeared at supper looking disheveled and wearing an old hat with decayed ostrich feathers, elbow-length gloves, and a mauve sequined dress, while Colin sported a top hat, a waistcoat, and leather boots that made him look like a cross between a Victorian banker and a cowboy.

"'Exploring,' I said, while Father shook with silent laughter.

"For a week we searched without success. But then one afternoon Colin came up to me while I was playing in the garden.

"'I found it,' he said in a hushed voice.

"'Let me see,' I replied equally quietly.

"Casting a glance back at the house, he pulled a large, antique-appearing key from his pocket.

"'Where was it?' I asked.

"'In the attic,' he replied. 'It was in this, hidden under a loose floorboard.'

"And he raised his shirt and extracted a black volume which he handed to me. I opened it cautiously. On the first page was a name—Luther Carlsfield—and two words—*noli legere*.

"'*Noli legere*?' I wondered.

"'Do not read,' Colin said, in that superior tone he used when he knew something and I didn't. 'It's Latin.'

"I flipped ahead. Lines of neat script flowed across yellowed pages.

Here and there a date was legible on the top of a page—16 August 1672. 25 September 1673—but of the writing, I couldn't make out a word.

"'What is it?' I asked.

"'I think it's a diary,' Colin said. 'At least most of it. But I only know a little Latin.'

"The book gave me an uncomfortable sensation, as if I was handling something unclean. I passed it back to him.

"'Luther Carlsfield must have been one of our ancestors,' I said. 'Father said there were some odd characters in our family.'

"Colin opened it to a page and pointed to a section set apart—like you see when someone quotes lines of a poem.

"'Look at this,' he said. '*Cave aperientem hanc portam*…Something about opening a door.'

"'*Qui aperit, cave.*' I read the next line. 'What does that mean?'

"He frowned. "'*Cave* is beware, like *cave canem*—beware of the dog. Whoever opens it, beware? Or, beware of opening this door?'

"'It sounds dangerous,' I said, thinking that the next words looked ominous: '*Qui interius habitat animas devorat.*'

"'Our very own mystery,' said Colin, who had always been attracted to the unknown and uncanny.

"I shivered. 'Colin, I don't like it. Maybe we should forget this.'

"'Where's your sense of adventure?' Colin chided, shutting the diary. 'You're just a scaredy-cat.'

"'Am not!' I said, feeling my temper rise.

"'Prove it on the next full moon.'

"'I will!' I said."

Cecilia smiled ruefully. "Colin always knew how to get me to do what he wanted. I regretted those words as the days passed and the night of the full moon drew closer, but what could I do? I was too prideful to admit that I was scared."

Cecilia rose and paced around the bench, her reddish hair flowing around her shoulders. I worked out a cramp from my leg.

"You could have pretended to be sick," I suggested.

She halted, leaning against the back of the bench. "I thought of that, but I was never good at acting. I didn't have any friends or relations I could visit. No, I was trapped. All I could do was try to appear braver than I felt.

"It was winter now, and snow fell all day long and well into the night. Colin could hardly contain his excitement—he was a bundle of barely restrained agitation all day long. I crawled into bed hoping that he would leave me alone and have his adventure by himself, but just after midnight there was a soft knock on my door.

"'Come on, Cissy,' Colin hissed, beckoning me through the opening.

"'Maybe the door won't be there,' I whispered back, but he gave me an annoyed look, and so reluctantly, I pushed back the sheets and followed him down the dim corridors. He was carrying the journal and the key. I paused to look out of an age-warped window at the fields of fluffy white, bright in the moonlight now that the clouds had blown past. The trees stood still and silent in their thick blankets, but the woodwork of the house creaked and groaned under the weight of the snow.

"'I looked up Luther Carlsfield in the library,' Colin said softly as we climbed the stairs. 'He was a weird one all right. Into alchemy and all sorts of strange things. He was fascinated by what might lie near us, but beyond our senses. He spent his life searching for a door.'

"'A door into where?' I asked, but Colin shook his head.

"'Most of his notes were burned after his death. But his journal was obviously missed—hidden too well, either by Luther himself or someone else.'

"'Someone who was afraid to burn it but didn't want it to be found?' I offered.

"Colin shrugged. 'Who knows?'

"We reached the second floor. Counted the doors.

"Five.

"My teeth chattered, and it wasn't because the corridor was chilly.

"We stood there for a moment. 'Well, go ahead,' I said. 'Don't keep waiting.'

"Colin held the diary up so that a shaft of light illuminated a page. He began to read.

"'*Habeo claveam et interius volo videre.*'

"'What did you say?' I asked, hating the tremor in my voice.

"'That I have the key and that I want to see inside,' Colin replied, closing the book and extending the key towards the lock.

"I fancied once again that I could hear the sound of distant screams."

Cecilia paused, and walked forward a few steps. I rose to stand beside her. Despite the fact that it was a warm day, I too felt cold. Just the way that Cecilia spoke brought a chill to me, also.

She cleared her throat. "'Are you sure you want to go in, Colin?' I said to him.

"He didn't reply, just gave me one of his goofy grins. Then he put the key in the lock. I thought maybe it wouldn't turn, but it did. The lock clicked back. Colin pushed it open, just enough to peek inside.

"'What do you see?' I asked, but again, he didn't answer. He pushed the door open a little farther, and sidled inside. I tried to peer past him, but he shut the door behind him. He was like that.

"For a moment, there was nothing. Then he screamed. It was a scream like I have never heard—a scream of such utter, complete terror, that for a moment I couldn't move. Blood-curdling doesn't describe it. 'Colin!' I yelled. Then I rattled the knob, but it was locked—and he'd taken the key in with him.

"Terrified, I turned and dashed downstairs. I fetched my parents—hammering on their bedroom door until they opened it.

"Cecila! What's the matter?" Father asked.

"'Colin's gone!' I cried.

"'What do you mean?' Mother gasped, appearing beside him.

"'Into the room—the fifth door!' I blubbered.

"I dragged them upstairs to the west wing. But when we got there, the door was gone. By now I was babbling incoherently—so incoherently that they called the doctor to give me a sedative."

Cecilia stopped to catch her breath.

"What was in there?" I asked, hardly daring to speak.

She shook her head, and her eyes were wide. "I never saw it. And, of course, no one believed me when I told them about the fifth door.

"No trace of Colin was ever found, despite my parents' frantic searching and the efforts of a small army of police that ransacked the house. There were no tracks in the snow outside, which the inspector in charge said was quite mysterious. I think he suspected that my parents had killed Colin and disposed of the body somehow, but that was quite ridiculous, and there was never a shred of evidence."

"It must have been awful," I said.

"Since then I've been an only child," she said in a curiously distant tone. She stroked her chin. "My parents couldn't stand to live there anymore, and we moved into a smaller cottage."

"And Carlsfield Manor was torn down?" I wondered.

She pursed her lips. "There was a fire just after we moved," she replied shortly. "It burned to the ground."

"A pity," I said.

"The fire department believed it was arson," she said, and the way she said it made me stare at her. She was gazing ahead, at the site where the house had stood. "Fire is supposed to be cleansing," she continued, her voice flat and uninflected, "but some people say you can still hear the screams."

Footsteps clattered on the pavement behind me, and I swung around. "Hello, Mrs. Stark," I said, addressing a smartly attired, middle-aged woman. "I'm sorry about your son. Cecilia was just telling me -"

The woman halted, her mouth open in mid-greeting, her cheeks reddened, then rounded on her daughter.

"Cecilia! You haven't -! How many times have I told you -!" She shook her head in exasperation, then grasped Cecilia's arm. "Home with you, right now!"

Finally, she spoke to me. "Forgive us, Arielle. I should have warned you."

"About what?" I asked, but too late, as Mrs. Stark pivoted her daughter and marched her briskly away. Cecilia glanced back over her shoulder to give me a slight smile—but in her eyes, did I see the glimmer of amusement or the glitter of madness?

Then they turned a corner and vanished from sight.

I remained rooted in place, still imagining the past and the events that

Cecilia had narrated to me. By now it was dusk, the streetlights were flickering to life, and the full moon was rising above the city skyline.

And faintly, so faintly as if originating from some distance, I heard a scream.

It must have come from one of the apartments.

Or perhaps it was only in my mind.

At least, I hope it was.

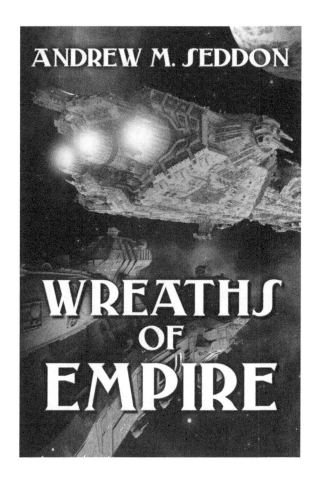

Wreaths of Empire, by Andrew M. Seddon

Naval Intelligence Commander Jade Lafrey retrieves a dying agent's last report from the wreckage of his ship, and stumbles into a conspiracy that may destroy any chance for peace between the Terran Hegemony and the alien Gara'nesh Suzerainty. The garbled message implies that someone is developing the ultimate weapon—but who? Together with her super-geek aide and an Information Officer she's not sure can be trusted, Jade must negotiate both the treacherous political starscape and the stirrings of her heart in order to avert catastrophe.

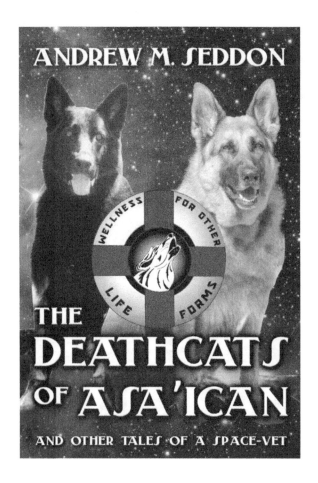

The Deathcats of Asa'ican, by Andrew M. Seddon
And Other Tales of a Space-Vet

The founder of WOLF—Wellness for Other Life Forms—Doc Hughes is a space-travelling exobiologist called upon to treat the most challenging cases in the colonized worlds. Accompanied by his telepathic German Shepherd Victrix, the alien skaggit Rex, and journalist Leina, Hughes encounters mystery, danger, and love among the stars.

Ring of Time, by Andrew M. Seddon
Tales of a Time-Traveling Historian in the Roman Empire

In the 27th century, humanity's greatest technological achievement is the massive, star-powered Temporal Displacement Ring: a portal to the past. Professor Robert Cragg, reeling from his own personal losses, volunteers to be the first-ever time-traveling historian, fleeing into the shadow of the Roman Empire. Instead of dry, dusty bygones, he encounters real people. Commoners and nobility, sailors and businessmen, zealots and legionaries, druids, gladiators and philosophers all cross his path. The past, he finds, is not dead and gone, but very much alive... alive with wonder, fear, and, perhaps, love...

Made in the USA
Monee, IL
22 January 2021

58421805R00121